Curtains for Love

Tim stared at Nikki. "But you have one of the leads in the play. If you felt you couldn't handle the pressure, you should have dropped out a long time ago."

Nikki's cheeks felt flushed and hot. How could Tim be so insensitive?

"Well, Lara is my understudy," she said icily. "Maybe I should drop out completely and let her take over the part."

"That's not what I—"

"Maybe you could spend even more time helping her rehearse," Nikki said. "Maybe you'd like that best of all." She opened the door and slid out of the car.

"Because obviously, Tim Cooper," she said, leaning back into the car, "I'm just not good enough for you—onstage or off!"

Books in the River Heights ® Series

Available from ARCHWAY Paperbacks

RIVER HEIGHTS #5

BETWEEN THE LINES

CAROLYN KEENE

AN ARCHWAY PAPERBACK
Published by POCKET BOOKS

New York   London   Toronto   Sydney   Tokyo   Singapore

AN ARCHWAY PAPERBACK *Original*

An Archway Paperback published by
POCKET BOOKS, a division of Simon & Schuster Inc.
1230 Avenue of the Americas, New York, NY 10020

Copyright © 1990 by Simon & Schuster Inc.
Cover art copyright © 1990 Doug Grey
Logo art copyright © 1989 James Mathewuse
Produced by Mega-Books of New York, Inc.

ISBN: 0-671-67763-2

First Archway Paperback printing May 1990

10 9 8 7 6 5 4 3 2 1

AN ARCHWAY PAPERBACK and colophon are
registered trademarks of Simon & Schuster Inc.

RIVER HEIGHTS is a trademark of Simon & Schuster Inc.

Printed in the U.S.A.

IL 6+

BETWEEN
THE LINES

1

"Nikki, I've got great news!" Tim Cooper said, his gray eyes shining. He took Nikki Masters's hand and pulled her inside the greenroom, the small, shabby room where the members of the River Heights High Drama Club passed their free time during rehearsals and performances.

Laughing, Nikki let herself be dragged along. She dropped onto the dilapidated tweed couch with a thump. Her blond hair flew into her eyes, and she blew it away. Her hands were filled with textbooks and her copy of the script for *Our Town*. "What's up?" she asked.

"Wait till you hear," Tim said eagerly.

Tim was playing George Gibbs in the River

Heights High production of *Our Town,* and Nikki was playing his sweetheart, Emily Webb. Everyone thought the two of them were a terrific combination, especially since Nikki and Tim were a couple offstage, too. Robin Fisher, one of Nikki's two best friends, said she'd be sure to get a seat at least three rows back—she didn't want to be hit by any sparks.

Nikki wasn't so sure that there was any danger. There were plenty of sparks flying between her and Tim, but Emily and George were a different story. Nikki was worried. The closer they got to opening night, the more unsure she felt about the simple things of acting—like remembering her lines and not tripping over her own feet.

Tim sat down beside Nikki on the couch, but he was too excited to sit still. He immediately sprang up and began pacing in front of her. "I just found out—not only is the drama critic from the paper going to review the play but WRH is doing a TV interview! Sheila O'Dell is going to interview you and me! Can you believe it?"

Nikki gulped. "Uh, no. I can't."

"Isn't that amazing?"

"It sure is," Nikki told him.

Tim stopped pacing for a moment. "You don't sound very excited."

"I am," Nikki said feebly. How could she

tell Tim that she didn't share his enthusiasm? He thought she'd gotten over her fear of publicity a long time ago. Nikki had thought so, too, for a while.

Well, she was over mere fright. She'd passed that point weeks ago. Now she was into sheer terror.

She couldn't tell Tim that, though. He thought that Nikki had really gotten her act together after Nancy Drew cleared her of murdering her boyfriend, Dan Taylor, the past summer. Tim thought she'd forgotten all those reporters and flashbulbs, the whispers and gossip. He didn't know that the sight of a video camera still sent her into a cold sweat.

Nikki tried to smile. "I'm just so nervous about the play, Tim. I'm afraid I'll forget my lines or trip—"

Tim waved a hand. "Hey, that's normal. Everything will be fine once you get onstage."

Nikki looked away. It was easy for Tim to say that. He'd had practically every lead in every play in every school he'd ever attended. He'd probably been the star of his nursery school.

Tim sat down next to her again and took her hand. "You're doing great in rehearsals, Nikki. Mrs. Burns thinks you're terrific. I think you're terrific. You won't fall apart on opening night."

"You want to bet on that?" Nikki asked.

"Absolutely." Tim leaned over and kissed her. "I'd bet on you anytime," he said softly.

Tim kissed her again. Nikki had just relaxed against him when the door banged open.

"What's this, an early rehearsal?" Kevin Hoffman shouted, barreling into the room. His red hair, which stuck up from his head in a frantic manner, clashed with his bright purple shirt. Kevin was obviously not afraid of attracting attention. Mrs. Burns had to ask him again and again to tone down his performance as the Stage Manager.

Kevin tried to squeeze in between Nikki and Tim. "I'm not interrupting anything, am I?" he said, half sitting on the very edge of the couch.

Nikki gave him a good-natured push and he landed on the floor. "What makes you think that?"

Kevin grinned up at her. He put a hand to his heart in mock surprise. "Do you mean I interrupted Nikki-Tim, not George-Emily? I'm a low-down dog, that's what I am."

"What you are, Kevin," Tim said, moving over on the couch to make room for him, "should be put between two slices of rye bread and served in the cafeteria for lunch."

Nikki giggled, and Kevin punched Tim lightly on the arm. "So I'm a ham. But, hey,

I'm just jealous. You know, having to compete with Laurence Olivier here."

"Give me a break, Kev," Tim said, embarrassed.

"I'm serious," Kevin said. "You're acting me right off the stage. I hate it. I mean, before you moved here from Chicago, Cooper, *I* was the star."

Nikki smiled faintly. Tim *was* a terrific actor, and superconfident, too. No wonder he was looking forward to extra publicity. Tim wanted the show to be a success so badly.

"Let's just hope enough people show up to see your performance," Kevin went on gloomily.

Tim straightened. "What are you talking about?"

Kevin shrugged. "I was just talking to Mrs. Burns. Ticket sales are down—way down. She's even worried about getting a full house for opening night."

That might not be too awful, Nikki thought hopefully. The fewer people there were to see her make a fool of herself, the better.

Tim frowned. "That's terrible! What if the press is there? How is it going to look? What happened to the old school spirit?"

Kevin ticked off the answers on his fingers. "Well, there's that exhibition basketball game, a big dance at Commotion—"

The door swung open wider, and Brittany Tate stepped into the room. "Not to mention," she said, "that nobody wants to see a fifty-year-old play that takes place in a cemetery."

"That's only the last act, Brittany," Kevin answered, scowling. Nikki knew that Brittany was hardly one of Kevin Hoffman's favorite people.

Brittany gave him a cool glance. "I know that, Kevin. I was just letting you know what people are thinking around here."

"Brittany, do you know that the green-room is for drama club members only?" Kevin asked pointedly.

"Press pass," Brittany said, smiling sweetly and waving her pad. Her dark eyes sparkled as her gaze fell on Tim. "I'm really looking forward to interviewing you tomorrow, Tim. Oh, and you, too, Nikki. I mean, if I can ever pin you down to a time."

Nikki's heart sank. Now Tim would guess that she'd been avoiding Brittany. The last thing Nikki wanted was to see her story splashed across the front page of the *Record*. She'd been putting the interview off for ages.

Tim shot Nikki a surprised look, then turned back to Brittany. "I'm at your service, Brittany. Anything to promote the play."

"*Anything?*" Brittany asked flirtatiously. Before Tim could reply, though, she added.

"You've been *so* cooperative, Tim." She gave a small sigh. "If only the rest of the cast was, too. My job would be a lot easier."

"Hey, you never even asked me," Kevin pointed out.

Brittany ignored him. No wonder, Nikki thought angrily. Brittany's remark had been directed at her—and it certainly hit home. Tim was frowning quizzically at her.

"Maybe Nikki should be interviewed with me tomorrow," he suggested. "That way you could get us both done at the same time, Brittany."

Brittany hesitated for only a fraction of a second. "Sorry, I have a strict rule about doing one-on-one interviews," she said firmly. "That's how I achieve that personal touch." She smiled at Tim again.

"How about after rehearsal today, Brittany?" Nikki broke in. She might as well get it over with—and she couldn't stand hearing any more snide remarks about her lack of cooperation. "I'll be free then."

"Are you sure?" Brittany asked, widening her dark eyes. "I mean, you told me how busy you were, being the star and everything."

The rat! Nikki had never said anything like that! "I'm not the star," Nikki said frostily. "And I'll definitely be there, Brittany."

"Great," Brittany said, tossing her lustrous dark hair behind one shoulder. "I'll wait for you in the auditorium, then." She swiveled around and returned her attention to Tim. "You know," she said eagerly, "I think some extra publicity in the *Record* might help increase ticket sales. The right article could really pull in an audience. I'll do my best."

"Thanks, Brittany. That'll be terrific," Tim said gratefully. He got a gorgeous smile in return. Nikki shifted uneasily. She knew that Tim loved her, but Brittany had been after him since the beginning of the school year. Nikki knew that Brittany would do practically anything to get him.

"Okay, guys." Brittany snapped her notebook shut with a satisfied air, although she hadn't written a single word in it. "Well, I've got a few things to take care of. Then I'll come back and sit in on rehearsal. That should give me some background information." She turned to Kevin and fleetingly touched his sleeve with a delicate finger. She trained her huge dark eyes on his. "I hear you're really terrific as the Stage Manager, Kevin. I'm looking forward to seeing your performance."

Kevin's mouth opened, then closed. Brittany could charm anyone, Nikki thought.

Kevin was still gaping when Brittany swung out of the room, her short, full red skirt swirling around her perfect legs.

Everything was clicking into place, Brittany told herself as she rushed to her locker. Finally!

Maybe she wasn't exactly at the pinnacle of the River Heights High social scene, where she'd been before all of her troubles. It had been one thing after another. That snake Jack Reilly had broken up with her, and her best friend, Kim Bishop, and Jeremy Pratt had cut her off at the knees for trying to put them together as a couple. Then she'd almost lost her star reporter status on the *Record*. She had told DeeDee Smith, the editor-in-chief, that there was *no way* she could get even a phone interview with the Dead Beats, the hottest new rock group around. Then that wimpy Lacey Dupree, alias the Mouse, had somehow gotten the group to make a personal appearance at the River Heights Mall! Brittany had barely pulled herself out of that one. Fortunately, she did manage to get a sensational interview and get it printed on page one. Karen Jacobs, who was her only competition for editor of the paper next year, had been absolutely livid.

Things were finally looking up. Kim and

Jeremy had another date for that very night. If all went well, Brittany was positive the two of them would sponsor her for a junior membership at the River Heights Country Club. And she'd just had a terrific brainstorm back there in the greenroom. If she wrote a dynamite article about the play for the *Record,* ticket sales would zoom. Not that she cared about *Our Town* all that much, but Tim Cooper did.

Brittany was definitely looking forward to that interview—alone—with Tim. It certainly was a challenge to pry that guy away from Nikki Masters. Those two were stuck together with glue.

As Brittany was taking her jacket and books out of her locker, Jeremy Pratt suddenly rounded the corner. There was a frown on his chiseled face, and when he saw Brittany, it got deeper.

"Where have you been?" he asked abruptly. "I've been looking for you everywhere."

Brittany controlled her irritation. Jeremy was a major pain, but until he sponsored her for the country club, she had to be nice to him. "I didn't know you wanted to see me, Jeremy," she said with a shrug. "What's up?"

Jeremy glared at her. "I have a date with Kim tonight."

"I know," Brittany told him. "Kim's real-

ly looking forward to it. Don't worry. You'll
do fine."

"I know that," Jeremy snapped. Then he
leaned back against a locker. "What I mean
is, I know that Kim likes me now—even
though you did your best to ruin everything
for us."

"I tried to *help* you!" Brittany said angrily.

Jeremy carelessly waved a hand. "Spare
me the excuses. Here's the bottom line: I
want a list of Kim's favorite foods from you. I
am *not* going to blow this date. I promised
her a moonlight picnic."

"A picnic?" Brittany said skeptically.
"Won't it be a little, uh, chilly for that?"

"It's been pretty warm lately, if you
haven't noticed," Jeremy said.

Brittany thought of brunches at the country club, the sexy bathing suits she'd wear to
the pool the next summer. "You're right,
Jeremy," she said. "It sounds like a fabulous
idea. So romantic." If you don't mind freezing to death, she added to herself.

"So what should I bring to eat?"

Brittany thought for a moment. She'd better be right or she'd never get what she
wanted out of those two. "Well, I'd go to that
gourmet catering place in the mall——"

"Tastings?"

Brittany nodded. "Right. Kim adores their
lobster salad. Let's see, you can pick up a

loaf of French bread there, and some Brie. Oh, and caviar—you know, to put on those little French crackers."

"Lobster and caviar? What are you trying to do, bankrupt me?" Jeremy complained.

"You can afford it," Brittany told him. "Don't forget dessert. One of those little chocolate mousse cakes, or a raspberry torte."

"Thanks for giving me some choices," Jeremy said sarcastically.

"Well, you asked for help. Do you want the evening to be a success or not?"

"I just don't know if I can trust you, Brittany."

She slammed **her** locker closed and twirled the lock. "Then why did you come to me, Jeremy? Go ahead, serve pastrami sandwiches and cream soda. See how well they go over with Kim."

Jeremy pushed away from the locker. "Okay, okay. But you better be right. If Kim and I don't hit it off, who knows if we'll agree on *anything*? Like sponsoring people for membership in the country club, for example."

Brittany held her breath. Jeremy was obviously going to keep her dangling as long as he could.

It killed her to do it, but Brittany smiled sweetly. "I see what you mean, Jeremy. Just don't forget the caviar. The most expensive kind, of course. Kim will know the difference."

She swept off, still smiling. Kim had had caviar once in her life, at a party her parents threw for some big shots from Chicago. Kim had raved about it, but Brittany had the feeling she wasn't as crazy about the stuff as she pretended. No way would Kim know the difference between cheap caviar and the expensive kind.

So much for Jeremy Pratt. Brittany's next step was to tackle Tim Cooper. Now, *that* was something to look forward to. She sighed heavily. If only Nikki Masters wasn't blocking her way.

2   ～～

Nikki missed her next cue. She'd watched Brittany enter the auditorium and take a seat in the front row. Her mind started to drift. What would Brittany try to do to her in the upcoming interview? Something, she guessed. It would be just like her.

Nikki should have been thinking about being Emily Webb, not about Brittany. She'd lost her concentration, just like that.

She knew her cue perfectly. In Act Three, right after the old woman talked about hymns, Emily was supposed to appear, wearing a white dress. She was supposed to be dead, of course, and she was to walk through the mourners to sit with the rest of the dead. Nikki had gone over and over with Mrs.

Burns what the effect should be, but she'd totally blown it.

Everyone was quiet, and the silence was awful. Even Mrs. Burns didn't say a word.

"Wake up, Emily," someone whispered from the wings. "You're not *that* dead." Another person snickered, and one of the mourners poked her in the back. Tim tried to look at her, but his head was bowed, since George Gibbs was supposed to be mourning his young wife, Emily.

Nikki finally walked forward, as she was supposed to, and sat down beside Lara Bennett, who played Mrs. Gibbs. She began to speak, but her missed cue had thrown her completely off. She couldn't get the rhythm of the scene, and Nikki began to panic. Lara was trying to help, giving her reassuring looks and trying to cover up the fact that Nikki had been slow to deliver a line. Finally Mrs. Burns called a halt.

"Nikki, may I see you down here for a minute?" the drama coach called. She beckoned with a thin arm, and Nikki heard her bracelets clank.

Uh-oh. Nikki had really messed up this time. Usually Mrs. Burns only called Kevin Hoffman off the stage for a conference.

Lara smiled at Nikki. "Don't worry," she said softly. "We're all pretty nervous."

"Thanks," Nikki whispered as she inched past her toward the stairs at stage right. She could feel everyone's eyes on her—especially Tim's—as she made her way toward Mrs. Burns.

Poor Nikki, Brittany thought, smiling to herself. Mrs. Burns sure knew how to embarrass people. She shifted her attention back to the stage. It was a perfect opportunity for her to observe the actors, and it was a rare chance to watch Tim without Nikki hanging all over him.

To Brittany's surprise, someone else was hanging over him now—Lara Bennett. Well, not *hanging* exactly—but close. Lara was leaning over Tim's copy of the script, her long brown hair grazing his shoulder. She was definitely standing nearer than she had to.

Brittany narrowed her eyes. She didn't know Lara Bennett well at all; she was surprised she'd even remembered the poor girl's name. She had pale brown hair and pale green eyes and pale skin and wore dull brown-toned clothes. Lara was only a sophomore, a year younger than Tim, and she acted young, too. A bit shy, a bit too eager to please. Not exactly competition for Nikki Masters, the sun goddess.

Or was she? Brittany sat up straighter. Was

that a flicker of interest in Tim's face? Lara was a good actress—she'd certainly been a lot better than Nikki that day—and Tim was crazy about acting. Sometimes a common interest could melt the ice. It would serve Nikki right if Lara tried to snare Tim. As long as she didn't catch him, of course. If anybody was going to pry Tim Cooper away from Nikki, it would be yours truly, Brittany Tate.

Wait until Nikki found out about Lara Bennett. Unless she already knew. Brittany frowned. Why else would Nikki be so out of it? Maybe that was why she'd been avoiding Brittany, too. Nikki didn't want her to guess why she was upset. Nikki knew Brittany had a real talent for sniffing out hot gossip. That was why Brittany was such a terrific journalist.

Brittany smiled again. Now, what could she do with this very interesting information about this odd little love triangle?

Brittany thought about the problem with the same concentration she brought to everything from choosing a new shade of lipstick to how long to wait before letting a boy kiss her. As always, the answer came quickly.

She had the perfect plan! Brittany snapped her notebook shut. There would be no interview that day after rehearsal, she decided right then.

Brittany gathered up her books and left her seat. She might have slipped up a bit lately. Nikki Masters had actually managed to come out on top in the last few skirmishes between the two of them, but Brittany was going to win the war. The first stage of the campaign would begin now.

The evening was perfect, crisp but not too cold. So much for that smirk on Brittany Tate's face, Jeremy reflected smugly. He had been right. The picnic was a fabulous idea.

At that time of year, Moon Lake was deserted. Jeremy pulled in and turned off the Porsche. Moonlight streamed across the dark water. Tall pines scented the air. Stars twinkled overhead.

"Nice," Kim said, nodding. "This might not be such a bad idea, Jeremy."

Well, she wasn't wildly enthusiastic, but for Kim, it was progress. Jeremy reached behind him for the soft wool blanket he'd swiped from his parents' bedroom. Then he quickly sprang out of the car so that he could open Kim's door.

As she slid gracefully out of the Porsche, Jeremy noted approvingly how great Kim looked in black corduroys, leather boots that laced to the ankle, a black turtleneck, a silver belt, and a short black leather jacket. Her blond hair fell in a gleaming straight line and shimmered against the black leather, and her dancer's body looked willowy and elegant.

"It'll just take me a few minutes to set up," Jeremy said as he spread out the blanket for Kim to sit on.

"All right." Kim tucked her legs beneath her and stared out at the lake.

Jeremy had planned every last detail. First, he went back to the car to get a linen tablecloth, which he spread out over part of the blanket. Then he hoisted out a cooler and hauled it over to the blanket. He ran back to the trunk to get the stemmed glasses he'd tucked away—crystal, of course. Then he poured Kim a glass of sparkling cider.

She took a sip. "Thanks. Could I have a napkin?"

"Sure," Jeremy said. He ran back and fished in the trunk for the linen napkins. Where were they? He tore through the rest of the items and spilled the salt. When he finally located the napkins and ran back to give one to her, Kim smiled her thanks and asked him to fetch another blanket. She was cold.

He ran back for that. Then Jeremy headed back to the trunk again to get the shopping bags from Tastings. He was starting to resent Kim sitting there doing nothing while he was running around. Kim was obviously used to being waited on.

"I think it's a full moon," Kim said dreamily.

"Mmmfff," Jeremy answered, his head in the trunk.

"It's such a beautiful night."

"Uh-huh." He pulled at the enormous wicker hamper. It weighed a ton. He yanked it out of the trunk, then staggered toward the blanket with it.

Kim sighed luxuriously. "Mmmm. This is so relaxing."

Jeremy only grunted in reply as he set down the hamper and fell onto the blanket. Well, at least everything was out of the car now. He could eat.

Kim looked around. "Didn't you say you brought your tape player, Jeremy? Some music would be great."

Jeremy swallowed a groan. "Sure. Don't move," he added, even though Kim had made no sign of moving an inch. Gritting his teeth, Jeremy headed back to the car again. Kim Bishop had better be worth all this hassle. Her nose might be a bit too pointy, he decided a little unkindly.

Dues!

Brittany threw herself on her bed and gazed up at the ceiling. Now that things were going so well, she'd almost definitely get that club sponsorship any day now. But she had one major problem. How was she going to pay the huge membership dues?

She'd thought about it before, of course, but she'd been too wrapped up in getting Jeremy and Kim to sponsor her to really concentrate on the problem. She just figured that somehow she'd find a way to get her father to pay them.

Now that the moment had almost arrived, she wasn't so eager to ask her dad. He had always said no to joining the country club. He was a wonderful person, but he had no idea what it took to get ahead socially. He didn't care, anyway. He'd rather sit around telling jokes with Tamara, Brittany's geeky younger sister, than chat with a corporate vice president. He was hopeless.

Brittany sighed and sat up. There was nothing to do but ask her dad straight out. There was no way she could lie about the money she needed. She couldn't say she wanted it for something else, like a fund-raiser at school or a new coat. It was too much money, and if he found out the truth, he'd kill her. Well, maybe he wouldn't kill her, but he'd be terribly disappointed in her. Brittany hated that worse than anything.

She swung her legs off the bed, gave a quick glance in the mirror, and started down the hall. Halfway to the living room she turned and ran back to her room to slip on the deep blue sweater that was her father's favorite.

The sweater didn't help this time. Sniffing into a tissue didn't help. Nothing helped. Mr. Tate shook his head, and Brittany's mother remained well hidden behind her magazine. Mrs. Tate always stayed out of the country club discussions.

"Can't do it, pumpkin," Mr. Tate said. "I'm surprised you'd even ask. We've been over this before. Those astronomical fees just to bat a few balls around a tennis court—"

"That's not it at all, Daddy," Brittany protested. "There are loads of things to do at the club—dances and parties. Plus *everyone* meets there on Saturdays."

Mr. Tate sighed. "And you go just about every Saturday yourself, Brittany. Why, you've been over there practically every weekend with Jack Reilly."

Brittany used the tissue to wipe away a nonexistent tear. "Oh, Daddy," she said with a throb in her voice. "You know that Jack and I broke up."

Mr. Tate looked distressed. "Oh, dear. I'm sorry, honey. I shouldn't have mentioned him."

Brittany peeked over her tissue at him hopefully. She sniffed one last time.

"But I still won't pay those dues."

Now real tears welled up in Brittany's eyes. She was so close! And all it would take was a little money. "Mom," she said hopefully, "what do you think?"

Mrs. Tate lowered her magazine. "Why don't you try to earn the money, Brittany?"

"You mean you'd give me more hours at the flower shop?" Brittany asked skeptically. She wasn't exactly turning cartwheels at the thought.

"Well, not right now," Mrs. Tate said. "It's pretty slow at Blooms this time of year. Things will pick up around the holidays, though."

"I can't wait until Christmas!" Brittany wailed. Who knew what might happen between Jeremy and Kim in all that time! They'd probably break up in a matter of weeks.

"I'm sorry, honey." Mrs. Tate appeared to be concerned, but she didn't offer any money, either.

Brittany turned and stomped back to her room without another word. She made a huge effort not to slam her door.

What was she going to do? She *had* to join the country club—and soon. Brittany threw herself back on her bed. She had to get another job, she thought glumly. It was the only way.

Tears slid down Brittany's cheeks. Her days were already so full of school activities and working at Blooms—not to mention shopping. How could she cram something else into her schedule? She'd never have time for dating now. It was just as well that Jack Reilly had broken up with her. That *toad*.

Brittany flipped over and lay with her cheek against her pillow. There was no use crying about it. She wasn't a privileged golden girl like Nikki, and she had to wait to be invited to every country club event by a member. She wasn't going to go through that humiliation anymore! She'd get a job—even if it killed her—and earn the money. If she collapsed from exhaustion, it would serve her parents right.

But, Brittany thought, sitting up and wiping her cheeks fiercely, first she would get Tim Cooper back. She'd taken him away from Nikki Masters once. She could do it again. If she was clever enough, in a matter of weeks she could have both the country club *and* Tim! Wouldn't that be worth any sacrifice?

Brittany bolted off the bed. She had some phone calls to make. First, Nikki.

She looked up the number in her address book, then punched it out on her phone.

"Hello?"

"Hi, Nikki, it's Brittany," she said breathlessly. "Listen, I am *so* sorry about having to leave today. Did you get my message? I told Kevin to tell you—"

"I got it, Brittany," Nikki broke in. "No problem."

"You're sweet. Look, here's the deal," Brittany went on quickly. "Since it's been so hard for us to get together, I was wondering if you'd do a phone interview."

"Right now?"

Nikki sounded just a bit panicked. Brittany grinned and reached for her notepad on the night table. "Would that be okay? It'll be short, I promise."

"I guess so," Nikki said slowly.

"Terrific. I really appreciate this, Nikki. I'm just swamped with work, and this will save so much time. Now, for the first question . . ."

3

When Brittany got to the greenroom before
classes the next morning, Tim was already
waiting. He looked terrific in a gray sweater
that matched his eyes. Way too terrific for
Nikki Masters, Brittany decided.

"Sorry I'm late," Brittany said breezily. "I
had to wait for my father to give me a lift."
Actually, Mr. Tate had had to wait for her.
The extra half-hour had paid off, though.
Brittany knew she looked sensational in her
short denim skirt, soft lavender sweater, and
low suede boots.

"It's okay," Tim said, checking his watch.
"But I have to meet Nikki before homeroom."

Brittany made sure her smile remained in

place. "This won't take long. Why don't we start? Lara seems to be a bit late."

"Lara?"

"I asked her to join us for the interview —I hope you don't mind."

Tim looked puzzled. "I thought you said that you only do one-on-one interviews."

Oops! Brittany thought fast. "Well, I don't have that luxury today. I have to get the piece in. It's the only way to boost those ticket sales, Tim," she added.

Tim nodded. "You're right," he said.

There was a timid knock at the door.

"Come on in, Lara," Brittany called, grateful for the interruption. Was Tim actually looking relieved that he didn't have to be alone with her? Brittany wondered.

Lara poked her head around the door. "Sorry I'm late. The bus took forever this morning." She inched into the room shyly, smiling at Tim. "Hi, Tim."

"Hi, Lara."

Not a great start, Brittany thought sourly. Tim was friendly to Lara, but that was all. This might not be so easy as she'd thought. Brittany stared down at her pad.

"Shall we start?" The other two nodded. "How do you feel about playing Tim's mother, Lara?"

Lara giggled, then blushed. "Well, Tim

makes it easy," she said. "He's such a terrific actor."

Brittany scribbled on her pad. "What about you, Tim?" she asked.

"I know what Lara means," Tim said, nodding. "Working with other people who are good can make your own performance better. When Nikki and I—"

Brittany gritted her teeth. "What about your scenes with Lara?" she broke in.

"Lara really gives her all," Tim replied. "I mean, you can just feel her emotion. She's terrific."

Finally! They were getting to the good stuff. Brittany took down every word, bending her head over her pad to hide her grin. The perfect plan was going to work— without a hitch.

Nikki was hoping to get an early copy of the *Record* the next morning, but she made it to homeroom just as the bell rang. She had to grab a copy from the teacher's desk as she walked out.

Brittany's article, "Behind the Curtain," was on the front page.

"See you at lunch," Tim told her as they paused outside homeroom. "I won't be in English today; I have a dentist appointment."

"Okay," Nikki answered, smiling. She felt more than a little nervous wondering what Brittany had written. She was dying to read the article, but dreading it at the same time. Nikki knew what Brittany was capable of and hoped she wasn't up to any of her tricks.

Tim gave Nikki a quick kiss on the forehead and walked off toward the south wing of the school.

"It sure *looks* like they're still together," Nikki heard someone say behind her.

Nikki spun around to see Ben Newhouse and his girlfriend, blond model Emily Van Patten. The two of them definitely looked uncomfortable when they saw Nikki. They quickly ducked into their classroom.

Who were Ben and Emily talking about? Nikki wondered. It sounded as if they were discussing her and Tim. But that didn't make any sense. Of course they were still together.

Frowning, Nikki scooted down the hall toward her trig class. As she rounded a corner, she waved to Lara Bennett. Lara was with a group of girls who seemed to be teasing her about something.

"Hi, Lara," Nikki called.

To Nikki's surprise, Lara blushed a deep red. "Oh, hi, Nikki," she said.

As Nikki hurried past the group, she could hear some of the girls whispering and giggling. A bunch of silly sophomores, Robin would say.

Then Nikki saw Jeremy Pratt and Kim Bishop moving straight toward her. Students were scurrying right and left to let the golden couple pass. Nikki smiled and said a quick hello as she approached them. Kim nodded, and Jeremy gave her his usual smirk. Why did they glance at each other and smile as she went by? Nikki wondered.

An uneasy feeling started creeping through her. What was going on?

Ignoring the whispers that followed her everywhere, Nikki headed straight to her usual table at lunchtime. She was glad to see that Robin and Lacey were already there with their boyfriends, Calvin Roth and Rick Stratton. She really needed some moral support.

Nikki slid gratefully into the seat that Rick held out for her. She didn't need to ask if her friends had read the article. They were all looking at her sympathetically.

"Let's face it, Nikki. Brittany Tate is a walking, talking disaster," Robin said flatly. She picked the tomatoes off her salad and gave them to Lacey, who slid them inside her ham sandwich.

"She shouldn't be allowed to write for the

Record," Lacey said, tossing her long red braid over her shoulder.

"That girl spells trouble," Rick agreed, shaking his head.

"Brittany blew me out of the water, all right," Nikki said. "The worst part of it is that I gave her the ammunition myself."

Robin pushed aside her salad and reached for Nikki's copy of the Record. She frowned. "I don't get it. Why was her interview with you so short?"

Nikki shook her head. "She called me and did the interview on the phone. All she asked me was if I was feeling nervous. She asked the question five different ways, and I answered it the same way each time." Nikki's eyes filled with tears. "I sound like an idiot."

Lacey took the paper from Robin and read a few lines of the article. " 'I guess I'm just nervous,' Nikki Masters told this reporter. 'You're up there on the stage all alone, and nobody can save you.' "

"Hey," Cal broke in, "what's so terrible about that?"

"Nothing," Nikki said mournfully, "but it gets worse."

" 'Lara Bennett had a different view of the perils of the acting profession,' " the article went on. " 'Sure I'm nervous,' she admitted. 'But a lot of people are depending on me.

Besides, all I have to do is look at Tim and I relax,' she told this reporter with a slight blush. 'He saves me every time.' "

Robin took the paper back from Lacey. "Tim Cooper agreed. 'I know what Lara means,' he said. 'Working with other people can make your own performance better. . . . Lara really gives her all—I mean, you can just feel her emotion. She's terrific,' he added with a warm look at his costar." Robin grimaced. "Yuck."

"That really doesn't sound too good," Cal agreed.

Nikki pressed her hand against her hot forehead. "I sound so stupid and selfish," she said. "Babbling on and on about *my* nerves, *my* fears, as if I don't care about anyone else or the play itself. And Tim and Lara sound like the greatest acting team since—since—"

"Fred and Wilma Flintstone?" Robin grinned.

Nikki felt too miserable to smile. "They sound like they're perfect for each other. And they don't even *mention* me. They talk about everyone else—Kevin Hoffman, Martin Salko, Mrs. Burns. It sounds as if they left me out on purpose."

"Whoa. Get a grip on yourself, Masters," Robin said sternly. She shook the newspaper at Nikki. "Remember who wrote the article, will you? Tim probably talked about you, and Brittany left those parts out."

"All of River Heights High is talking about this article," Nikki said grimly. "I'm sure of it. Is Tim Cooper breaking up with Nikki Masters? Are Tim and Lara Bennett an item?"

"Well, don't let Brittany see you all upset," Lacey said. "Have some lunch."

"I can't," Nikki said, shaking her head.

"Brittany deserves major retaliation," Robin announced, wrestling with a plastic packet of salad dressing. Finally she got it open, and the dressing spurted out. Robin leaned back quickly, and the arc of dressing missed her by inches.

Everyone laughed, but Nikki only smiled faintly.

"Go ahead, laugh," Robin said, examining the man's tweed vest she was wearing over her orange T-shirt. "This is from an old suit of my dad's. I love it and wouldn't be too happy to have it all splattered with Russian dressing." She dipped a piece of lettuce into the pool of dressing that had landed on the table.

"Ugh," Lacey said, shuddering. Her freckled nose wrinkled in distaste.

Calvin grinned. "Nice going, Fisher," he said.

"Now, back to that revenge I was talking

about," Robin said. "I'll think of something, Nikki. Don't worry. Uh, Nikki?"

Nikki jumped. "Oh. Sorry. I was just thinking."

Lacey gave Nikki a curious look. "You're awfully jumpy these days. I've never seen you like this. I mean, well, not since . . ."

"I know," Nikki broke in. "Since I was accused of Don Taylor's murder."

"You've got to get a grip on yourself," Robin advised briskly.

Rick put an arm around Nikki's shoulder. "Listen, Nikki. I admit this isn't the greatest article for you, but at least everyone's talking about the play."

"It *is* good publicity, Nikki," Lacey agreed.

"Terrific," Nikki said glumly. She picked up the *Record* and read the last line of Brittany's article. " 'So what's *really* going on in *Our Town?* Tune in opening night for the answers.' " She tossed the paper aside.

"You see?" Robin said, shaking her fork at Nikki. "Everybody'll be there opening night. I bet it'll be standing room only. The whole audience will be waiting to see if you push Lara Bennett off the stage."

"I'd rather push Brittany Tate out a window," Nikki said. "Or maybe Tim will. He must be furious."

"All the rumors will die down by this

afternoon," Lacey said firmly. "I mean, it's ridiculous. Tim and Lara Bennett? Come on."

"That reminds me," Nikki said. "Where *is* Tim?"

Suddenly Calvin looked uncomfortable. "Oh. I guess I forgot, Nikki. I ran into Tim as he was leaving the building to go to his dentist appointment. He asked me to tell you that he couldn't meet you for lunch today."

"Why not?" Nikki asked, surprised. "Was his appointment going to run late?"

Calvin looked even more uneasy. "Well, not exactly. He's, uh, going over some lines."

"Why do you look so weird, Cal?" Robin prodded.

Foreboding filled Nikki's heart. "Who is he rehearsing *with,* Cal?" she asked.

"Who?" Calvin cleared his throat. "Actually, it's uh——"

"Out with it, Cal," Lacey demanded.

Calvin looked down at the table. "Lara Bennett," he said.

4

Brittany picked at her food. Kim was boring her to tears with her tenth recital of every minute and every detail of her date two nights before with Jeremy. Her low, confessional tone had caused any visitors to their table to walk away after a quick hello. To make matters worse, Samantha Daley was hanging on to Kim's every word, her light brown eyes envious. It was so disgusting. Brittany didn't know how she'd be able to keep her lunch down.

Although Samantha herself usually only toyed with boys, lately she'd been showing a more romantic side. Now she was exclaiming after every detail Kim revealed.

"Then he brought out the caviar," Kim said. She gave a tiny yawn.

"Caviar?" Samantha repeated in her slight southern drawl.

"And that fabulous lobster salad from Tastings——"

"I'd die!" Samantha's accent was getting more pronounced with each exclamation.

"And he said I was the most beautiful girl at River Heights High——"

"I'd *die!* Wouldn't you, Brittany?"

"I've heard it before," Brittany said. Then she remembered that she and Kim were involved in a still-shaky truce. "Not from Jeremy, though. He doesn't give many girls compliments. You must have swept him off his feet, Kim."

Kim shrugged. "I think so. Anyway, then we looked at the moon, and we held hands——"

"What an amazing date!" Samantha said.

Brittany rolled her eyes. Now that the country club junior membership was sewn up—except for the small matter of the dues, of course—she was totally bored with the Jeremy-Kim romance. The two of them could sit around admiring each other's cheekbones for the rest of the school year for all she cared.

"Are you and Jeremy going to opening night of *Our Town?*" Samantha asked Kim. "Everybody is."

Brittany sat up straighter. Here it was—

a perfect opportunity to change the subject.

"I suppose so," Kim said with a shrug. "Jeremy wants to, and people would probably wonder why we weren't there."

Brittany stifled a groan. As soon as she officially got her country club membership, she'd have to start thinking of ways to break up the Kim and Jeremy Show. It was obvious that Kim now thought she was running the River Heights High social scene.

Kim played with her empty soda can. "I was thinking of Le Saint-Tropez for dinner before the play. I think I'll tell Jeremy tonight."

"Le Saint-Tropez? That's incredibly expensive," Samantha said. She shook her cinnamon curls back off her face. "I'd die," she said again.

Brittany couldn't stand it another second. "Before you die completely, Sam, you might want to hear some gossip. It might revive you."

Samantha ignored Brittany's sarcasm and leaned over the table to hear the gossip, her eyes glowing. Kim looked interested, too, though she tried not to show it.

"On my way to the cafeteria," Brittany said in a whisper, "I saw Tim Cooper and Lara Bennett in the greenroom. You couldn't have put a hair between them."

"You're kidding!" Samantha gushed. "Is it all over between Tim and Nikki?"

Brittany controlled a strong urge to empty her cottage cheese and pineapple salad over Kim's perfect blond head. "Oh, I don't think so—not yet, anyway," she said airily. "Anything could happen."

"What are you planning?" Samantha asked eagerly.

Brittany put a finger to her lips. "I can't say anything yet, but I have a major surprise for Nikki Masters."

Kim looked bored. "I wonder where Jeremy is," she said. "I wanted to talk to him about tonight. We're supposed to have dinner at the club."

Brittany took a huge bite of salad so that she wouldn't scream at Kim to shut up. She hated that Kim got to be driven around in a Porsche, but the next night she would be on a bus, traveling to a sleazy section of River Heights. She'd seen an ad in the paper for a waitress job at Slim and Shorty's Good Eats Cafe. It sounded horrible, but at least she wouldn't run into anyone she knew in that part of town—and she needed money for her dues—fast.

Digging furiously into her salad, Brittany decided that there was only one consolation. Kim Bishop might have a ride in a

Porsche and a date at the country club, but she had to go with Jeremy Pratt.

As Jeremy drove through the streets of River Heights that night with Kim, he reminded himself that he'd always wanted a girlfriend with class. He'd known that dating Kim would mean shelling out a lot of cash. It was just that he hadn't expected it to cost quite so much.

Now Kim wanted to go to Le Saint-Tropez for dinner before the play! That would set him back almost a hundred dollars, at least, he thought, pulling up at a red light.

Still, Jeremy thought as he glanced over at Kim sitting poised and perfect in the passenger seat, he really shouldn't complain. He had the car. He had the girl to go with the car. He had the looks, he had the money. He couldn't expect it to come without a price. Most of the price would be picked up by his dad, so what was he worrying about?

Jeremy gunned the engine and took off from the light like a thoroughbred from the starting gate. Kim's head was back, her lips curved in a dreamy smile. Jeremy shifted into second. Life was pretty good, he thought.

Just then the Porsche made a horrible noise. It began to buck like a horse in a rodeo. Jeremy turned the wheel and eased the car to the side of the road. It hit the curb and stopped dead.

Kim looked annoyed. "What is it?"

Jeremy knew very well what it was. The transmission had just fallen out, or whatever transmissions did when you put off fixing them. His mechanic had warned him it might happen. He'd said he had to have at least three days to fix it, but Jeremy couldn't bear the idea of leaving his car in the shop for three days.

"It sounds like transmission trouble," he said casually.

A thin line appeared between Kim's perfectly arched eyebrows. "Transmission trouble? Isn't that pretty serious?"

"Not at all," Jeremy lied. "I have an excellent mechanic. It'll be no problem."

Kim settled back in her seat with a satisfied air. "That's good to hear." She stared straight ahead through the windshield.

"Uh, Kim?"

"Yes, Jeremy?"

"The car isn't going anywhere now. I have to get help."

Kim bounced up. "And leave me sitting here? Are you crazy, Jeremy Pratt?"

Jeremy sighed. "Come with me, then. I'm sure there's a phone booth a few blocks from here."

Kim peered out through her window. "I don't like this neighborhood."

"Come on, it's not that bad," Jeremy said wearily.

"It certainly is," Kim said. "I'm wearing heels and my good silk jumpsuit, *and* we have reservations at the club."

"What do you want me to do, Kim?" Jeremy asked irritably. "I can't fix the car. Look, are you staying here or what? I don't have all night."

Angrily, Kim jerked her car door open. "All right, I'll come with you. I'm not sitting in this car on a dark, deserted street, that's for sure."

"Fine." Jeremy got out of the car and came around to take Kim's arm, but she shook him off.

"I can walk perfectly well, thank you."

Jeremy ignored Kim and thought about his Porsche. His father was going to blow his top when he found out about this. He'd always said that an expensive car needed to be babied. He'd be furious that Jeremy had allowed the problem to get out of hand.

If only this had happened when he was with one of his buddies or by himself. Why did Kim have to be there? She only made things worse.

There was no phone on the first block or the second. Kim's mouth was pressed in a thin line. She didn't say a word. Then, in the middle of the third block, it started to rain.

Tim and Nikki were driving home from rehearsal in silence. The rain pattered lightly on the roof of Mrs. Cooper's Taurus. Tim fiddled with the radio at first, then shut it off in exasperation.

"I just don't get it," he burst out suddenly. "I thought Brittany's article was great. Everybody's talking about the play now."

Nikki sighed. They'd started to discuss this before rehearsal, but Mrs. Burns had called them onstage. Their argument hadn't helped their scenes one bit. Then rehearsal had run late, and now they were both tired and hungry. Nikki knew it wasn't a great time to have a fight.

"Tim," she said in a reasonable tone, "can't you see what Brittany did? She made it sound as if I couldn't care less about the play. She practically came right out and said that you and Lara were crazy about each other."

Tim frowned. "Come on, Nikki. Don't you think you're exaggerating just a little?"

Nikki shook her head. "No, I don't. Because at least a dozen people asked me how our rehearsals were going."

"So?"

"So," Nikki said patiently, "they had this

funny look on their faces. Like they knew something I didn't."

"Let them talk." Tim shrugged. "Who cares? We know we're together."

"But everyone else thinks that you and Lara—"

"Come on, Nikki, Lara doesn't mean anything to me. I told you that Mrs. Burns wanted us to go over that scene together." Tim lowered his voice. "Nikki, I love *you*."

Nikki sighed. "Oh, Tim, I love you, too. But—"

"Then why are you so upset?" Tim exploded. "Brittany did a great job of drumming up interest in the play. You know I'm no big fan of hers, but this time you're way off base. I'm sure Brittany had no idea her article would be interpreted like that."

Nikki couldn't believe it. "Are we talking about the same Brittany Tate here, Tim? *You're* the one who's off base, and I'm sick and tired of giving that girl the benefit of the doubt. I've done it too many times, and I just end up looking stupid. Of course she knew what she was doing."

Tim squinted through the slashing windshield wipers. "You're really acting crazy, Nikki. And now your performance is falling apart, too."

"I know." Nikki felt like bursting into tears. Tim had always been so sensitive. She could go to him with her smallest problem, her stupidest fear. Now he didn't understand her at all. What was happening to them?

"You were doing so great before," Tim said, sounding slightly baffled. "Sometimes we'd be onstage, and I'd feel like I *was* George Gibbs and you were Emily Webb. I didn't get that feeling out of thin air, Nikki. I got it from you."

"I know, Tim," Nikki said softly. "I felt it, too."

"Now, a little more than a week from opening night, you're starting to fall apart! You're scared stiff onstage, Nikki. You're not flubbing your lines, but you're not feeling them anymore."

"I'm trying," Nikki whispered.

Tim pulled into the Masterses' driveway. "The thing is, Nikki, you're throwing everyone else off, too. A cast is a team. Without you, the whole play could be a flop!"

"Tim, please! Stop piling pressure on me!" Nikki stared miserably at the raindrops snaking down the car window.

Tim turned off the ignition and sighed. "I'm sorry, Nikki. I didn't mean to get you more upset. I guess I got carried away. It's just that this play is so important to me. You understand, don't you?" He took Nikki's hand and linked his fingers through hers. "Can't you tell me what's going on?"

Nikki looked down at their entwined fingers. She tried to gather strength from Tim's firm touch, the feel of his palm against hers. "I think it started when all this publicity stuff kicked in," she confessed. "And now we have that WRH-TV interview with Sheila O'Dell Friday night. . . ."

Tim nodded. "But, Nikki, you have one of the leads in the play. You must have known this would happen. If you felt you couldn't handle the pressure, you should have dropped out a long time ago."

Tears started to slip down Nikki's cheeks. Fortunately, the car was dark so Tim couldn't see. "Maybe you're right," she said.

"Nikki, I didn't mean that the way it sounded. Look," Tim said gently, "I understand about stage fright. I've felt it myself plenty of times. I'll probably be just as nervous as you on opening night. Hey, we're only amateurs. But that doesn't mean we shouldn't try to act like the pros. Do you know what I mean?"

"Sure," Nikki said in a small voice.

Tim glanced out his window. "I was talking about this with Lara this afternoon. She agrees with me completely."

Nikki sat up a little straighter. Her tears seemed to dry up instantly. "Oh, she does?"

Tim nodded. "And look at Lara's performance. Remember how her voice shook at the audition? She was like a little scared rabbit. It's amazing she was able to get up the courage to go onstage at all. But Mrs. Burns saw something in her and took a chance. Now Lara's doing great, but underneath it all, she's scared to death—she told me so."

Nikki's cheeks felt flushed and hot. Anger rushed through her in a wave. How could Tim be so insensitive?

"Well, Lara is my understudy," she said icily. "Maybe I should drop out and let her take over the part."

"That's not what I—"

"Then you could spend even more time helping her rehearse," Nikki said. She couldn't stop the words from tumbling out of her mouth, even though she knew she must be hurting Tim. "Maybe you'd like that best of all." Tears were threatening to spill down her cheeks again, and Nikki swung her head to peer out the window. She fumbled with the door handle.

"Nikki—"

She opened the door, feeling cold air rush in. As Nikki slid out of the car, rain pelted her cheeks. She leaned back into the car.

"Because obviously, Tim Cooper," she said, "I'm just not good enough for you— onstage or off!"

Nikki slammed the car door and ran across the wet grass. Sobbing, she hurried up the front steps and fiddled with her keys. Behind her, Tim's car started and slowly drove away.

Jeremy shifted his leather knapsack from one shoulder to the other. Kim was fifteen minutes late picking him up. Now he'd be late for homeroom. For once, he would have preferred the bus. He just hoped Kim wasn't still furious about their date last night. They'd both gotten soaked, and she'd insisted on going home immediately. The only transportation he had been able to find was in the cabin of the tow truck.

But she *had* insisted on going to school with him this morning. It would be bad for them to be seen apart, she'd said. Jeremy supposed she was right.

He hoped Kim was in a better mood now. His day was already going badly. Over breakfast, his father had informed him in no uncertain terms that he wouldn't pay to fix Jeremy's Porsche. In fact, Mr. Pratt had hit the ceiling when he heard that the problem was the transmission.

Jeremy was thinking so hard that he didn't notice Kim pulling up to the curb in the old white Mustang she had just been given by her parents. She tapped the horn, making him jump.

"You didn't have to blow the horn at me, Kim," he said as he opened the door and slid in.

Kim gave him a cool glance. "We're late," she said curtly. She pulled away from the curb with a squeal of tires.

"That's not my fault," Jeremy said. "Slow down, will you? You want to have an accident? Then we won't have any wheels at all."

Kim shot him a quick glance. Her blue eyes were as warm as Moon Lake in February. "What does that mean? Won't the Porsche be fixed soon?"

Jeremy stalled. "I'm not sure yet," he said. "I'll talk to my mechanic this afternoon."

"Well, I was hoping it would be fixed by tomorrow," Kim said, frowning slightly. "We've been invited to two parties this weekend. It'd *better* be done by next Friday. I made reservations for an early dinner at Le Saint-Tropez before the play."

Jeremy's heart sank. A transmission job *and* an expensive French restaurant. He'd never be able to afford this. Maybe it would be easier just to break up with Kim.

But when they pulled into the school parking lot and Jeremy saw everyone on the quad turn to look admiringly at them, his spirits rose.

Jeremy and Kim got out of the car. Mark Giordano, the River Heights High football center, gave them a wave.

"Lookin' good!" he shouted to Jeremy. Then he turned back to the group of admiring girls surrounding him.

Jeremy gave Mark a thumbs-up sign. Then he took Kim's hand. They were still furious at each other, but there was no sense letting the whole school know.

"Be firm with that mechanic, Jeremy," Kim said, keeping a smile on her face.

"Yes, ma'am," Jeremy muttered. He waved to Ben Newhouse and Emily Van Patten.

They swept up the walk. Jeremy noted each admiring glance, each whispered comment. Even the seniors seemed to respect them. How could he break up with Kim, now that they were practically king and queen of River Heights High? He'd *have* to fix the Porsche, and soon.

When they reached Kim's locker, she kissed him lingeringly on the lips in front of everyone. Then she had to rush off to find Samantha Daley. Jeremy kept a smile on his face as she left. Actually he was tempted to do something completely childish—like stick out his tongue at Kim's retreating back. A girlfriend sure made life complicated. He headed toward his locker.

"Hey, pal." Hal Foster came up behind him. His sunglasses were pushed down to the end of his nose, and he looked over them at Jeremy. "You look lousy. What's up?"

"Nothing," Jeremy snapped. "Are you expecting the sun to go into nova, Hal?"

"Huh?" Hal's hand flew to the sunglasses. He scowled and removed them. "Just asking a friendly question, Pratt. Excuse me for living." He pushed past Jeremy to open his own locker.

Jeremy didn't bother to apologize. He reached inside his locker for his trig book. "The Porsche dropped its transmission last night," he said. "You know what that means."

Hal whistled. "Major bucks. Bummer."

"Oh, it's not so much the bucks," Jeremy said. He couldn't tell Hal that he was broke; the news would be all over River Heights High by second period. "My mechanic says he can't fit me in."

"So get another mechanic." Hal shrugged.

Jeremy shook his head. "No one's touching my car but Alfie. My father's been going to the guy for years."

"So what's Princess Kim going to ride around in while you wait?" Hal asked with a grin. "I mean, her Mustang's a few years old."

"Knock it off, Hal." Jeremy slammed his

locker shut and looked at his watch. "Come on, we'll be late for homeroom."

"Too bad you don't have wheels," Hal said as they headed toward the stairs. "There's a big poker game at the club tomorrow night. It's that prep school crowd—very high stakes. I guess it's better you don't have wheels."

"Yeah." Jeremy shrugged, but his mind was working fast. A big-money poker game might be a good way to earn some quick cash.

He'd have to cancel his date with Kim. Maybe a convenient case of stomach flu could strike him. Kim probably wouldn't be very sympathetic. If he didn't have the Porsche in working order soon, though, she could put him out of commission for real.

 **5**

Brittany had no trouble finding Slim and Shorty's Good Eats Cafe Thursday night. It was on the edge of town, right near the river. Once she found the place, she almost got right back on the bus and rode home again.

The building was tiny with peeling white paint and a pink neon sign that read Good Eats. It looked especially seedy in the pouring rain. As soon as Brittany opened the door, the odor of grease from hamburgers almost made her ill.

At least the place was packed. That meant good tips. Brittany shook out her umbrella and dumped it in a milk can by the entrance.

She saw a small man in a white jacket scurry past her toward the kitchen. She ran after him a few steps. "Shorty?" she called.

"Yeah?" The gruff voice came from behind and surprised her.

Brittany turned. A man slowly unfolded himself from a stool at the counter. Brittany looked up and her eyes met his belt buckle. She tilted her head back. This man was *tall*.

"Shorty?" she asked uncertainly.

"Yeah. Need a table?"

"No," Brittany said, flashing him a smile. "Actually, I need a job. I hear you're looking for a waitress."

He nodded expressionlessly. "Let me get my partner." He leaned over the counter and bellowed in the general direction of the kitchen. "Slim!"

Brittany wasn't really surprised when a small, pudgy man ran out of the kitchen. He had a wooden spoon in his hand. "What?" he shouted irritably.

Shorty jerked his thumb toward Brittany. "She wants the waitress job."

Slim made a face. "She don't look very strong. Can she carry a full tray? Better give her one and see if she can lift it, Shorty. And try her out on a full order, okay? I gotta get back to my chili." He turned abruptly and hurried back through the swinging doors.

"Don't worry about the trays," Shorty said. "I don't expect you to carry heavy ones. Make two trips if you have to. You saw

Raoul, the busboy. Just give a holler for him."

"Thanks," Brittany said gratefully.

Shorty tossed her a pad and pencil. "Take down this order. Two cheeseburger platters. One medium rare, with raw onions, pickles, lettuce, tomato. One rare with grilled onions, no pickles, lettuce, tomato on the side. Two orders fries, two coffees, one black, one cream. One BLT, hold the mayo. One iced tea. One lemon meringue pie." Shorty rattled off the order so rapidly that Brittany barely had time to write down a shorthand version of it. Luckily she was used to taking fast notes during interviews.

"Read it back," he said.

Fortunately Brittany had an excellent memory. Only occasionally glancing at the pad, she took a deep breath and spit back the order as fast as Shorty had given it to her.

He looked at her, obviously impressed. "You're not as dumb as you look, kid."

Brittany gritted her teeth. "Thanks. Do I have the job?"

Shorty nodded. "You have the job. Stay out of Slim's way, and you'll do fine. We just opened the place six months ago, and he's a mite nervous."

Brittany put all her charm into her smile. She wanted to be on the good side of the boss from the very start. "Okay. Thanks, Shorty."

"Don't mention it. Save the smile for the customers, kid. Three nights a week, start at five o'clock, and the lunch shift on Saturdays. Your first shift is tomorrow night, so don't be late."

"I won't," Brittany promised. She felt elated as she pushed open the door and stepped out into the cool air. She could probably still fit in a few hours at Blooms every week. She had a better-paying job now—in a noisy, crowded greasy spoon with two very weird bosses. At least she was actually going to make some money, though.

The next morning Brittany sat on the school bus, trying to screen out the chatter around her. Riding the bus was a pain. Even though she was past missing Jack Reilly, sometimes she still missed his car.

Brittany was staring out the window when suddenly she felt someone standing over her seat. She didn't bother turning her head. She didn't usually greet anyone on the bus—most of the other passengers were freshmen and sophomores.

The shadow at her shoulder didn't move. Finally Brittany turned irritably to confront the nervous green eyes of Lara Bennett.

"Hi, Brittany," Lara said hesitantly.

Brittany opened her mouth to reply in a way that would let Lara know she was in no mood for conversation. Then she remembered her plan. She patted the seat next to her.

"Hi, Lara. Have a seat."

"Really? Oh. Gosh. Okay." Beaming, Lara sat down.

"How are things going?" Brittany asked.

Lara settled back into the seat with a happy wriggle. "Okay, I guess. I mean, the play's going well."

"I'm not talking about the play," Brittany said meaningfully. "What about Tim Cooper?"

Lara's face turned bright crimson. "Oh. Well, I guess things are the same."

"I hear that Nikki and Tim are barely speaking," Brittany prodded. She hadn't heard that, but . . .

"That's not true," Lara said. "Tim drove Nikki home from rehearsal last night."

"But I bet he'll be giving *you* rides home pretty soon," Brittany said.

Lara blushed again. "I wouldn't say that."

Now Brittany was even more annoyed. Would this mushy-mouthed sophomore ever get her act together? If Lara didn't get Tim away from Nikki, how could Brittany get him away from Lara? She was perfectly happy to give Tim to Lara for a while. Lara would be a pushover; Brittany could get rid of her in three minutes flat.

Lara wasn't cooperating, though. Brittany eyed her. The girl wasn't bad looking. She just needed a few beauty tips—and a very large push.

Brittany sighed loudly.

"What's the matter, Brittany?" Lara asked. "Are you okay?"

Brittany twisted in her seat and lowered her voice. "Listen, Lara. I shouldn't really tell you this, but . . ." She let her voice trail off as if she couldn't bear to go on.

Lara's eyes widened. "What is it, Brittany?"

Brittany took a deep breath. "Look, Tim and I are very close. He's always told me things. He and Nikki have been having problems for a long time."

"Really?"

"I probably shouldn't say this," Brittany went on in a low, thrilling voice. "But I think you should go for it."

"Go for what?" Lara asked breathlessly.

What an idiot! "For Tim," Brittany said, trying not to sound impatient. "I can tell when he likes someone, Lara. And he likes *you."* Brittany sighed again. "Poor Nikki. She'll be upset, I guess. But anyone can see why Tim would be interested in you, if you'd just give the guy a chance. He's always talking about what a great actress you are. Haven't you noticed the way he looks at you?"

"Well," Lara said slowly, "no, not really. But my friends have. Ever since that article, they've been saying that Tim wants to ask me out."

"Well, they're right!" Brittany said as the bus pulled into the River Heights High parking lot.

Lara looked down at her lap. "I don't know, Brittany. I *do* kind of have a crush on Tim. But Nikki is so gorgeous. She's like the prettiest girl at River Heights High." She glanced up at Brittany quickly. "I mean, except for you, of course."

"Mmm." Brittany tried to control her irritation. "Why don't you come over Saturday morning and I'll help you with your clothes and makeup? You know, we can look through magazines, fool around with hairstyles, that sort of thing."

"That'd be great!" Lara said breathily. "You'd really do that for me?"

"Sure," Brittany said, gathering her books. Why not? She'd fix that limp hair of

Lara's and maybe suggest a good haircut. And she might give her a lesson in how to flirt. She wouldn't teach her everything, of course. Brittany had to save some of her best secrets for the day she went after Tim Cooper herself.

 **6**

That Friday night, Chip, Wes, Bob, and Tad welcomed Jeremy into the poker game.

"Sure, old man," Chip said. He undid the brass buttons on his navy blue blazer. "Just a friendly game. We're always glad to have another player."

"Have a seat," said Tad.

"Can I get you a drink?" Wes offered.

"A root beer's fine," Jeremy said, feeling a little uneasy. These guys were only a year older than he was, but he felt out of his league. Still, he was a fairly sharp card player, and he had scraped together a hundred dollars to bet with. If he was lucky— and he felt very lucky—he could win enough in one night to get the Porsche fixed and take

Kim to dinner. If she was still speaking to him. As Jeremy had expected, she hadn't taken the news of his sudden stomach flu very well.

He took a seat at the round table in the club's private room. The other guys had obviously just come from the dining room. They carefully removed their striped ties and jackets and hung them on the backs of their chairs. Jeremy took off his own tweed jacket. He hadn't eaten at the club; he couldn't afford it. He'd had dinner at home, then walked over.

"We go to Talbot," Chip said conversationally as he picked up the cards. "But I think I've seen you around the club. Where did you say you went to school?"

"River Heights High," Jeremy mumbled.

"Oh." Chip looked bored.

"Public school," Wes said to no one in particular.

Jeremy wasn't used to being patronized. He wasn't about to take it, either. "I like it," he said. "How is it going to school without girls?" he asked pointedly.

"Dismal," Tad said.

Chip motioned Jeremy to cut the cards. "I remember now. I've seen you hanging out here with some gorgeous blond. Is she your girlfriend?"

Jeremy gave a slight nod. "Kim."

"Very hot," Wes said approvingly.

"Very," Chip agreed, starting to deal. "Way to go, Pratt. I admire your taste."

Jeremy took a swig of soda and felt himself cheering up. True, he'd been nervous about crashing this game—Hal had hinted that these guys were a rough crowd. They weren't so bad, though. Jeremy picked up his cards and felt even better. A good hand. He made a substantial bet.

He won that hand and then the next. Jeremy began to relax. This just might work. By the end of the evening, he could be rolling in dough.

Nikki's room looked as if it had been blown up. Clothes were thrown on the bed, the floor, and the desk. Red, orange, green, blue, polka dots, and stripes gave the room a circus atmosphere. Nikki sat on the floor with her chin in her hands as Robin continued to pull dresses out of her closet.

"Hey, I've never seen *this* before," Robin said. She pulled out a short pink dress. "It's cute. Sort of."

"I wore it when I was eleven," Nikki said. She sighed. "I think you're coming to the end of my wardrobe, Robin. You'd better make up your mind soon. I can't be late for this stupid TV interview."

"It takes time to find the perfect outfit,"

Robin said, frowning as she examined a deep green pullover. She was wearing black leggings and a black-and-white striped top, but in the last half-hour she'd added Nikki's orange scarf, a paisley vest, and a pink miniskirt, which she'd pulled on over her leggings. As a final touch, she'd put on Nikki's gray fedora.

"At this rate, I'll have to go in my bathrobe," Nikki grumbled.

"Okay, okay," Robin said distractedly. She threw the pullover aside and began rooting through the clothes on the bed. "It's not just the audience you want to impress. You have to knock Tim's eyes out."

"Forget it," Nikki said gloomily. "Since our fight, he's hardly looked at or spoken a word to me."

Robin pushed aside some clothes and sat on the edge of the bed. "Nikki, you've got to snap out of this. You can't let Brittany spoil everything."

"I'm not, Robin," Nikki said wearily. "It's not just Brittany's article anymore. It's everything. I'm nervous, I'm jealous, I'm ticked off, and I'm messing up in rehearsals. I'm doomed."

Robin slid off the bed and thumped down next to Nikki on the floor. "What's happened to your self-confidence, girl? You're like a bowl of cold mush."

"I don't know," Nikki said. "I seem to have lost it somewhere."

"Well, until you find it, fake it! You're going to be on TV tonight!"

Nikki felt a sudden wave of panic shoot through her. The TV interview with Sheila O'Dell. "I'm scared, Robin."

"Scared? Why?"

Nikki shook her head. "Last summer, after Dan Taylor's murder, all those reporters were always around me, sticking their microphones and cameras in my face. They just kept pushing and shoving and yelling questions at me. Where was I the night he died, did I do it—all that kind of stuff. Then somebody asked if Dan had broken up with me before he was killed, and I almost went crazy. I was so scared. And when I saw the tape on TV, I sounded so mean and cold! I looked like a cold-blooded murderer." Nikki bit her lip. "If Nancy Drew hadn't cleared my name, I don't know what would have happened."

Robin's big, dark eyes were full of concern. "Oh, Nikki, I'm so sorry. I didn't realize—"

Nikki smiled faintly. "It's okay. I can handle this interview, I guess."

Robin squeezed her hand. "You'll do just great. I know it."

Nikki looked at her watch and jumped. "Oh, no! Mrs. Burns will be here soon. She's driving Tim and me to the TV station." She felt desperate as she looked at the sea of clothes. "Maybe I should just wear my jeans."

"Hang on." Robin began to rummage through the clothes on the bed, throwing most of them on the floor. "Don't worry, I'll clean all this up. I just thought of the perfect thing. It's under here someplace."

Robin dug out Nikki's red turtleneck dress. "Ta-da! Here it is! You'll *have* to be confident in red."

Robin pulled Nikki to her feet. In three minutes flat, she had zipped her into the dress, found shoes and panty hose, and dug up a wide black suede belt. She rummaged through Nikki's jewelry case until she found a pair of black jet earrings that had belonged to Nikki's grandmother.

Nikki peered at herself in the mirror. She had to admit the outfit was sensational. At least she *looked* sure of herself. "Thanks, Rob," she said. "You came through, as usual."

Mrs. Masters knocked softly and stuck her head inside the door of the bedroom. She shuddered slightly when she saw the mess, but her green eyes warmed when she saw Nikki. "You look beautiful, honey," she said. "Tim is downstairs. Mrs. Burns is waiting in the car."

"Okay, Mom." Nikki took a deep breath.

"You'll do just fine," her mother said reassuringly. "Your father and I will be watching."

"Me, too," Robin said. "I'm going to clean up this mess and then head over to Cal's. Lacey and Rick are meeting us there. We'll all be glued to the TV."

"Great," Nikki said faintly. She picked up her purse. Fake it! she reminded herself. She squared her shoulders and strode out the door.

Jeremy was losing. Badly. He couldn't believe it. With each hand, he was sure his luck would change, but he continued to lose. He was starting to sweat.

The other guys were perfectly cool— maybe because Jeremy was losing the worst. Chip had a wad of bills in front of him, and Wes's pile wasn't too bad either. No one said a word, except to bet.

Jeremy lost another hand. He pushed his remaining cash in Wes's direction. "Well, that's it for me, guys," he said, trying to sound cheerful.

"You can use an IOU if you want to keep playing," Chip said offhandedly. "We trust you."

"Oh." Jeremy thought quickly. Did he have the guts to keep playing?

Chip looked up as he dealt the cards. He paused in front of Jeremy's place, his fingers tapping the cards impatiently.

Maybe just a few more hands. His luck *was* going to change. "Deal me in," Jeremy said. He reached for his cards.

Nikki screwed her eyes shut against the bright lights. Her heart was pounding.

"Open your eyes, Nikki," Sheila O'Dell said gently. "They'll adjust to the lights in a minute."

Nikki blinked. They were sitting at a small table in the middle of the studio, waiting to go on the air live. After a minute she could make out the crew behind the cameras. Nikki concentrated on breathing normally.

She couldn't blow this. Not after what had happened with Brittany. Nikki knew that most of River Heights High would be watching the broadcast.

Tim leaned toward her. "You look great," he whispered.

"Thanks," Nikki said softly. She and Tim hadn't had a chance to say much to each other so far. First Mrs. Burns had chattered all the way to the station. Then there had been a whirlwind of technicians and people dabbing makeup on their faces. Nikki wasn't even sure if Tim was still angry with her.

Sheila O'Dell looked up from the notes on her lap. She smoothed her frosted hair and straightened her collar "Don't be nervous, kids," she said briskly.

Someone called for quiet. Sheila O'Dell looked toward the camera, a prepared smile on her face. Behind the camera, a young woman counted down from ten on her fingers. Nikki swallowed hard. *Fake it!* her mind screamed as the red light on the camera winked on.

Chip raked in the pot and gave a long stretch. "Another hand?"

"Sure," Tad said.

Bob yawned. "I guess."

Jeremy stood up. "Deal me out." He reached for his jacket. "Got to get home."

"Sure, old man," Chip said. He picked up the pad on which he'd kept track of Jeremy's IOUs. "Let's see," he said, running his pencil down a column of numbers that seemed impossibly long to Jeremy. Chip scribbled a figure at the bottom of the pad and pushed it toward Jeremy. "That sound about right?"

Jeremy almost fell on the floor in shock. He added the figures quickly in his head. The total was correct. "Sure," he managed to croak.

"So. You meet us here tomorrow and give

us the cash, right?" Chip pushed a shock of straight dark brown hair off his forehead and fixed his clear green eyes on Jeremy.

Jeremy began to feel nervous. "Okay," he said. "But I, uh, might have a problem coming up with the cash that quickly."

"Whoa. I don't like the sound of this," Wes said, rising. Jeremy noticed for the first time that Wes was very large, with an impressive set of muscles beneath his monogrammed white shirt.

Chip put out a hand, and Wes instantly sat back down. "Maybe I should explain, Pratt," he said amiably. "It's a matter of honor to pay your gambling debts. This could have very serious consequences."

"I *will* pay them!" Jeremy said. "I just don't have the cash. I mean, not right now."

Chip gave Jeremy a cool glance. "This changes things, doesn't it?" he said.

"You bet," Bob said. He was completely awake now, his small eyes mean and hard.

"Doesn't look good, Pratt," Tad said. He clenched and unclenched a hamlike fist.

Jeremy felt slightly sick. "I—I could give you something as collateral," he stammered, "like my watch, or—"

Chip waved his hand carelessly. "No way, Pratt. Cash only." He looked around the table. "We're very particular about that. We hate it when somebody stiffs us."

"Well, sure. I can see that," Jeremy said, thinking frantically. The door was on the other side of the table. He'd have to get past all four guys to reach it. He had a feeling they weren't going to step aside politely.

"Of course, there's always . . ." Chip's voice trailed off.

"What?" Jeremy asked eagerly.

"That gorgeous babe of yours. Kathy."

"Kim," Jeremy said weakly. Now he really felt sick.

"Kim. I might be willing to forgive the debt, if I had a date with her."

Wes dug his elbow into Chip's side and snickered. Chip didn't laugh. His glittering green eyes were very serious. Jeremy felt cold, looking into them. He wouldn't trust this guy with Kim for a second.

"No way, Chip," he said quietly.

Chip rose as swiftly and smoothly as a cat. "That's too bad, old man. That really is too bad."

He started around the table toward Jeremy —and the rest of the preppies came with him.

7 ～～

Jeremy moved fast. He vaulted over the table, scattering cards and money, and rolled off the other side. He felt fingers grabbing for his shirt. Then he heard it rip. He made the mistake of turning for just a second and met Bob's fist coming toward him. Jeremy ducked, and the blow glanced off his cheekbone. Somehow he managed to get the door open.

A group of middle-aged men looked up and blinked at him. He was in a room at the club reserved for chess and backgammon.

Jeremy smiled. He was very glad to see them. "Good evening, gentlemen," he said.

Chip's voice was low and deadly behind him. "We've got your number, Pratt."

Jeremy turned and mustered up his dignity. "I'll be in touch," he said, "old man."

Chip's expression didn't flicker. Jeremy tucked his torn oxford shirt into his pants and left, breathing rapidly. Except for a stinging cheekbone and a torn shirt, he was intact.

When Jeremy hit the cool air of the parking lot, he started to run. There was no sense taking chances.

He didn't have far to go, but he'd left his jacket behind. By the time he reached home, he was chilled to the bone.

He stood under the chandelier in the front hall for a few minutes, listening. At this time of night his parents were probably sound asleep, but he decided to play it safe. Jeremy didn't want to run into his dad, looking the way he did. If Mr. Pratt ever found out his son had lost money gambling, Jeremy would be grounded until college.

There was no sound downstairs, so Jeremy headed quietly up to his bedroom. He breathed a sigh of relief when he saw no light underneath his parents' door at the top of the stairs.

Alone in his room, Jeremy sat on the bed, a blanket around his shoulders, and considered his fate. He was in hock to four prep school goons. And he didn't have a penny to his name.

Jeremy knew what he had to do. He had to get a job.

Grimly, he shrugged off the blanket and slipped downstairs again. The evening paper was still lying on the leather chair in his father's study.

He took the paper back up to his room and surveyed the want ads. The Loft was looking for a waiter, but no way was Jeremy going to work there. It had to be a place where no one could possibly recognize him.

Then he saw it—an ad for a dishwasher. Jeremy was surprised to learn that a dishwasher could be a person and not an appliance, but he thought he could handle the work. At least he'd be in the kitchen where no one would see him. And the restaurant was all the way on the outskirts of town. Jeremy considered this for a moment. Could he really work in a place called Slim and Shorty's Good Eats Cafe?

"One last question," Sheila O'Dell said.

Nikki felt her stomach unclench. It was almost over! She hadn't done too badly. In fact, she thought she'd done pretty well.

Ms. O'Dell smiled gaily at both of them. Then she trained her keen blue eyes on Nikki. "I've heard through the grapevine that you two are a couple offstage as well.

Does that make things easier or harder in rehearsals?''

Instantly, Nikki's stomach knotted up again. What a question! How should she answer? She shot a look at Tim, her eyes pleading with him to save her.

Tim sailed right in. "I'd say a little of both, Sheila," he said, smiling. "Wouldn't you expect that?"

Ms. O'Dell looked a little taken aback at being asked a question herself, but then she laughed. "I suppose I would," she said. "Thank you, Nikki Masters and Tim Cooper. And good luck Friday night in *Our Town.*"

Nikki and Tim thanked Sheila O'Dell and waited while she turned back to the camera and gave the dates and times of the performances. Then the bright lights switched off.

"You were fabulous, kids," Sheila O'Dell said, removing her tiny microphone. "I wish all my interviews were that easy." She waved and stepped off the set.

Nikki turned to Tim. "Thanks for jumping in on that last question," she said. "I didn't know what to say."

"I know," Tim said quietly.

Nikki wished Tim would apologize for the other night. Or maybe she wanted to apologize to him; she wasn't sure. All Nikki really knew was that she wanted things to be the way they were before.

They both spoke at the same time.

"Tim—"

"Nikki—"

The two of them laughed. "You first," Nikki said softly.

"I'm sorry about the other night," Tim said. "I know I get really involved in the play. But nothing's more important to me than you. Not even acting."

"And nothing's more important to *me* than you," Nikki said.

"We have to keep remembering that," Tim said. "We can't let the pressure get to us."

"I know," Nikki agreed softly.

Tim took her hand, and they walked out to the reception area, where Mrs. Burns was waiting. Nikki's heart felt lighter than it had in weeks. What Tim said sounded so simple.

But as the three of them pushed open the door and headed into the cold parking lot, Nikki shivered. It did sound simple, but dress rehearsal and opening night were fast approaching. Next week would be the hardest of all.

When Brittany opened her eyes on Saturday morning, she still felt tired. Reaching underneath the blanket, she gingerly felt one foot. How could both feet still hurt from last night? It seemed unbelievable that she'd have to get up and wait on tables again.

She must have been temporarily insane to invite Lara over that morning. All she wanted to do was sleep until she had to go to work.

She would try to comfort herself with the thought of all the tips she'd stashed in her sock drawer. Brittany had been shocked when she reached home last night and emptied her greasy pockets. At this rate, she would be able to pay the first installment of the junior membership dues in a couple of weeks.

There was a knock on Brittany's door. Mrs. Tate came in and stood by her bed. "Hi, sweetie," she said, peering down at her worriedly. "I thought I'd check on you. You looked so tired last night."

Brittany sat up and pushed back her hair. "Thanks, Mom. But I'm fine. Just a little tired. A friend of mine is coming over in a few minutes."

"Oh? Kim?"

"No. Someone else. Actually, not really a friend. It's this sophomore who's been following me around. I promised I'd help her with her clothes and makeup."

Mrs. Tate nodded. "That's nice of you, honey." She reached over and pushed a strand of hair off Brittany's face. "I just want to tell you that your father and I are very proud of you for getting a job, Brittany. We know how hard you're going to have to work. I hope you can handle it all."

"No problem, Mom," Brittany said brightly. If her mom started worrying, she might make her quit, and that couldn't happen! "I'm going to *like* working, really."

"Well, you let me know if it gets to be too much for you." Mrs. Tate gave Brittany a hug. "Now, go on downstairs, I made chili omelets for breakfast."

Brittany gave a deep shudder. "Please, Mom," she moaned. "Don't make me eat chili."

Mrs. Tate laughed. "Okay. I'll bring you up a doughnut and a glass of juice. You take a nice long shower. I'll send your friend up when she comes."

Brittany dragged herself off the bed. It was nice to know her parents were proud of her, but right then, she'd rather have had the cash.

Brittany leafed through a magazine while she munched her doughnut, trying to picture which hairstyle would magically take Lara from overlooked to looked over.

A tentative knock on the bedroom door signaled Lara's arrival.

"Come on in," Brittany called. As soon as Lara walked through the door, Brittany held up the magazine. "You could look like this," she said, pointing to a brunette model in a short purple dress.

Lara took the magazine. "You really think so?"

"Sure," Brittany said. "All you need is a little bit of nerve."

"I don't know," Lara said skeptically.

"Lara," Brittany said impatiently, "if you have enough nerve to get up on a stage, you have enough nerve to change your style—*and* go after Tim Cooper. Especially when I tell you exactly how to do it."

A small smile played around the corners of Lara's delicate mouth. Something flashed in her eyes—the same inner determination that had pushed her up onstage and won her the part of Mrs. Gibbs.

Brittany grinned. "That's more like it." She took Lara's arm and pulled her toward the closet. "Come on. We're about the same size. Let's find a new look for you. Tomorrow Tim is going to have the surprise of his life."

She hummed a tune to herself as she tossed clothes to Lara to try on. Tim would be surprised, all right. And so would Nikki Masters.

8 ⌇⌇

On Monday morning, Jeremy waited outside his house for Kim. He turned up the collar of his jacket in the wild hope that it would conceal the bruise on his cheekbone.

"Hi, beautiful," he said as Kim pulled up a few minutes later. He slid into the car.

"Hi," she said coolly.

Kim was still angry at him for deserting her over the weekend. Jeremy sighed and gazed out the window. Even if she missed the bruise, she'd nail him when he tried to get out of taking her to Le Saint-Tropez Friday night. Now that he'd gotten the job at Slim and Shorty's, he'd somehow have to dodge Kim three nights a week and Saturday afternoons.

At least he'd been able to get time off next Friday. He could still take Kim to the play, but he had to work in that greasy ptomaine palace until six-thirty. Shorty hadn't been crazy about letting him off early his first week at work, and Jeremy was going to have to work a double shift on Saturday to make it up. He'd have just enough time on Friday to change and make it over to Kim's to pick her up in his mother's car.

If only he could simply tell Kim he was absolutely broke. Unfortunately, he couldn't just walk up to a girl like Kim and say, "By the way, would you mind eating pizza and watching TV for a few weeks until I can afford to take you out again?" He'd be out in three seconds flat. At this point Jeremy was beginning to wonder if that would be so terrible.

"I went shopping," Kim said conversationally as she stopped at a red light. "I found the perfect dress for Le Saint-Tropez."

This was it. It was now or never. "Uh, about Le Saint-Tropez . . ." Jeremy began. His voice trailed off as Kim fixed her sharp gaze on his face. Her eyes lingered on his cheekbones.

"Jeremy! What's that?" she asked.

Kim was staring at Jeremy's face. Was that a bruise on his perfect cheekbone? "What happened to you?" she asked.

Jeremy turned his head away. "What are you talking about?"

At the next light Kim moved his chin back so he faced her again. She touched his cheekbone, and he winced. "Right there. It looks black-and-blue."

"My mother opened the door in my face," Jeremy told her. "It's fine. It'll go away, all right? The light turned green."

"Okay, okay," Kim answered huffily. She stepped on the gas harder than she meant to. For heaven's sake, she was only trying to show some concern. Why was Jeremy so jumpy?

"How are you feeling?" she asked, giving it one more try.

"Better, but I was sick all weekend. It was gross. You don't want to hear about it," Jeremy said.

Kim's ice blue eyes narrowed. If this was what having a steady boyfriend was like, she didn't think she liked it. She'd spent the weekend all alone, too. She'd been embarrassed to go to the parties they'd been invited to without Jeremy. She didn't know if she totally believed Jeremy when he'd announced he had a stomach flu. If only he hadn't looked so *healthy* when he'd said it.

As she pulled into a space in the school parking lot, Kim told herself that if she didn't like the idea of being a couple with Jeremy Pratt, she could dump the guy. She wasn't willing to give up yet, though. Because of him she'd been asked to more parties than ever before—one of them given by a senior. She was even making Brittany jealous. Everything was going great—except that Jeremy was acting so weird.

Kim took his arm as they walked toward school. She could see that everyone was watching them, as always. "I hope you got the tickets for *Our Town,*" she said. "I hear opening night is sold out."

"I got them," Jeremy said.

"Now, what were you going to say about Le Saint-Tropez? Wait until you see my new dress."

"Oh, yeah. Le Saint-Tropez . . ." Jeremy began. He cleared his throat.

Kim stiffened as she scented trouble. She'd told everyone they'd be going there before the performance. He'd better not try to weasel out of it. "Yes, Jeremy?" she asked edgily.

"I thought my parents were going to Chicago this weekend," Jeremy said. "They're not."

"So?" Kim shrugged. "I wasn't exactly expecting them to join us. Though I'd love to meet them sometime."

"Well, it's my mother's birthday. We're having a dinner party for her at our house Friday night, so—"

"Oh, I see. That's all right, Jeremy." Kim pictured the Pratt house with the tall columns in front, the elegant dinner that would be served. She could still wear her new dress. "I'd love to come. We can do Le Saint-Tropez some other time."

Jeremy looked startled. "No!" he burst out. Then he caught her eye and smiled nervously. "I mean, that'd be great, Kim, but the party's for family only. It's my father's rule, not mine."

"I see," Kim said. Was Jeremy lying? He wasn't looking away guiltily; he was staring right into her eyes. For some reason, though, she didn't believe him.

Jeremy pressed her arm against his side. "When you meet my parents, I want to make it a special occasion. It'll be *your* night, Kim."

"I see," Kim said slowly. "Well, maybe we can go out somewhere after the play. Everybody's going to the Loft."

"Sounds great!" Jeremy squeezed her arm again. "I'll get to show you off. You'll wear your new dress anyway, won't you?"

"Sure," Kim said. She felt a bit better, but not much. If Jeremy Pratt was lying and making a fool of her, he'd be extremely sorry.

She'd give him one more chance to shape up.
Then she'd show him what dating Kim Bishop was all about.

After school Nikki, Lacey, and Robin
raced to the auditorium.

"You guys are so great to be helping me
out," Nikki said.

"Are you kidding? This'll be fun," Lacey
said. "It's like dress-up when we were kids.
We'll help you with your costume and hair
and makeup. You'll look great on opening
night."

"Are you sure Sasha won't mind?" Robin
asked as they reached the auditorium.

Sasha Lopez was in charge of costumes for
the play. She'd done a fabulous job with the
clothes in the drama club's wardrobe room,
improvising whenever needed.

"It's okay," Nikki said. "Actually, Sasha
suggested I get some friends to help. She's
swamped, I guess."

Nikki led Robin and Lacey through the
maze of corridors in back of the stage. Mrs.
Burns was running over light and sound cues
with the stagehands while the actors had
their final costume fittings. Backstage was a
madhouse. Students were tearing by, some
carrying chairs from the set; others had their
arms full of turn-of-the-century costumes.
Kevin Hoffman was trying on the hat he was

wearing as the Stage Manager. Martin Salko, dressed in his costume as Howie Newsome, snickered when Kevin leaned over and snapped his suspenders.

Robin backed up to avoid running into a stagehand and bumped into Nick Maudners. "Have you seen my glasses?" he asked her.

Nikki and Lacey burst out laughing. Nick gave Robin a disgusted look and rushed off again.

"Nick is in charge of lighting," Nikki explained to Robin. "I don't know how he lost his glasses."

"Oh," Robin said in a small voice. "Maybe you should show us where the costumes are. It's probably safer in the dressing room."

"Follow me," Nikki said, heading toward the wardrobe room. It was crowded with actors either looking for their costumes or badgering Sasha to take up a hem or sew on a button.

"I'm supposed to have a pink dress," Karin Todd wailed. "I look awful in green."

Sasha pushed at her spiky black hair. Normally she had a quirky sense of humor, but that day she looked frazzled and unhappy.

"See if Cheryl Worth will trade dresses with you," she told Karin distractedly. "She's wearing pink. And you two are about the same size."

"We are not," Karin said huffily. "She's a size nine."

"But she's a *small* nine," Sasha said soothingly. When Karin turned away, Sasha rolled her eyes and consulted her clipboard. "Next?"

Lara Bennett appeared, the long black dress she would wear for the third act in her arms. "Sasha? Did you take up this hem?"

Sasha shook her head. "Not yet. Try it on with your padding first."

"Oh, right." Lara scurried away.

Wordlessly, Nikki, Robin, and Lacey watched her go.

"Did you see that?" Nikki whispered finally.

"I'm afraid so," Robin gulped.

"Lara looks so—different," Lacey said slowly.

"Different?" Nikki said. "She looks *gorgeous!*"

"Not gorgeous," Robin said quickly. "But definitely, uh, good."

Lara Bennett had gotten a haircut. Her soft brown hair was now chin length, straight, and shining. It set off her fair, creamy skin. She was wearing makeup for the first time, too. Her pale lashes were suddenly visible, lush and long under a light coat of brown mascara. Her eyes looked like pale green emeralds. She was wearing an oversize sweater in the same green, black leggings, and flats. She looked fantastic.

What could this transformation mean? Nikki stifled a groan. She knew exactly what it meant. Lara was going after Tim, and she wasn't going to be subtle about it, either.

"I can't believe it," Nikki said wonderingly. "Lara was so—so—"

"Mousy," Robin said. "Pretty, but let's face it, mousy. Maybe she went to the mall and got a makeover. I'd like to know where she went. I'd go there myself."

A flush stole over Lacey's pale face. "I bet I know exactly where she went," she said. Her voice shook with anger. "Or rather, to *whom.*"

Realization dawned in Robin's dark eyes. Nikki felt pain knife her near the ribs. They all exchanged glances.

"Brittany Tate," they said together.

Brittany pushed through the swinging doors to the kitchen, balancing her tray on her hip. Slim had given her a cheeseburger order with fries when she'd specifically asked him for potato salad. Last week she would have been nervous about approaching him, but it hadn't taken her long to realize that Slim's bark was worse than his bite. She wasn't afraid of setting foot inside the kitchen anymore.

She waited while Slim rattled the baskets of sizzling fries. He wouldn't be able to hear her now, anyway. The new dishwasher was hauling a rubber tub of dirty dishes back to his station, which was behind a partition. Brittany frowned. She couldn't see the dishwasher's face, but there was something familiar about the way he moved.

Impossible. How could she know anyone in this dump? Brittany studied the guy. He looked like a dishwasher, she supposed, but he was wearing expensive top-of-the-line athletic shoes.

Then the dishwasher turned to go behind the partition, and she glimpsed the famous Pratt profile.

Brittany almost dropped her tray right on the grill. *Jeremy Pratt!* What was he doing here?

9 〜〜

"You catching flies, kid?" Slim asked Brittany.

Brittany closed her mouth. "No," she said dazedly. "Sorry." She turned around and bolted through the swinging doors. Then she leaned against the wall near the counter.

What was Rich Rat Pratt doing working as a dishwasher?

That didn't matter right then. Eventually he was going to see her, and then what could she do? She didn't want to look for another job. Sure, she had grease spots on her uniform and she had to wear horrible shoes and it took her twenty minutes of soaking in a hot tub to get the cheeseburger smell off her skin. It wouldn't be for long, though, with all her tips. Why did Jeremy Pratt have to come along and ruin everything?

Janice, the other waitress, came up behind her, balancing a full tray. "Table three is getting antsy over there, Brittany. If I were you I'd look sharp before Shorty notices."

"Oh. Thanks, Janice." Brittany picked up her tray again. Janice was older and had four kids. She was often tired and grumpy, but she watched out for Brittany. Brittany talked table five into taking french fries instead of potato salad and went to get iced tea for table nine. As she filled the glasses, she wondered if she could possibly avoid Jeremy completely. He worked behind a partition. The dishwasher was supposed to help bus tables, but if she was quick and cleaned up her own, he'd never have to leave the sink.

If she knew Jeremy, he wouldn't last long as a dishwasher. He was too lazy.

Brittany went back to the question of why Jeremy needed to work in the first place. Actually, this might make a very interesting piece of gossip. As long as Jeremy didn't find out she was working there as well, of course.

Brittany scanned the room. There were several tables that needed to be bused. She headed for the kitchen for a tub to help Raoul. On the way, table five called to her.

She had to run and get them ketchup and mustard. Table six wanted another order of fries, and table two filled up with six new customers. Brittany tried to hurry them along. Behind her, she practically heard the dirty tables screaming for Raoul and Jeremy. What could she do? He'd see her for sure now!

Jeremy felt the tips of his ears burn as he ducked his head and scrubbed frantically at a pan.

Brittany Tate! What was she doing here?

If there was ever anyone he wouldn't want to hold his life in her hands, it was Brittany. If she found out he was working here, she'd spread the news all over school in a matter of minutes. What if she told Kim? He'd be dead meat.

Brittany hadn't seen him, he knew, but what was he going to do now?

Jeremy set the pan in the drainer to dry. It wasn't bad enough, he fumed, that he had to stand over this steaming water with his hands in creepy rubber gloves, scrubbing away at layers of grease. It wasn't enough that he had to dump other people's disgusting leftovers into a garbage can and be yelled at every five minutes by that jerk Slim. Now he was going to be publicly humiliated!

Brittany would have no mercy.

"Hey, kid!" Slim yelled. "Get out there and clear some tables!"

Jeremy stuck his head cautiously around the partition. "I'm busy," he said.

Slim turned slowly, his meaty hands on his pudgy hips. "You *like* your job, kid?"

Jeremy ducked back and stripped off his rubber gloves angrily. How could people ever stand to work at jobs like this? If he ever got out of there alive, he vowed he'd never sink into debt again.

Jeremy peered out through the swinging doors. Brittany was taking an order at a far table. He grabbed one of the gray tubs used for stacking dirty dishes and ran out into the dining room, keeping his face hidden.

Working faster than he ever had in his life, Jeremy filled the tub with the dirty dishes. There was a tip on one table. He was tempted to pocket it, but he knew Brittany would race back into the kitchen to grill Raoul about it. Right then she was sticking her pad back in her pocket and turning away from her table.

Jeremy quickly hoisted the tub of dishes onto his shoulder to hide his face and ran back to the kitchen. He shouldered the doors open and skidded to a halt, breathing hard.

"Whew," Slim said as he cracked eggs into a bowl. "That was pretty fast, kid. Maybe you'll work out after all."

* * *

Lara Bennett practically flew up the steps of the school bus Tuesday morning. Debbie Johnson and Darlene Parker, her two best friends, had saved her a seat.

"Is that a new jacket?" Darlene asked enviously, leaning over the aisle toward Lara. "I've never seen it before."

Lara nodded. "I got it last night. Mom loved my new haircut, so she came through with some new clothes, too."

"Great," Debbie said. She looked slyly at Lara. "Did Tim notice your haircut at rehearsal yesterday?"

Lara dropped her voice. "Well," she said, "he didn't *say* anything, but you know how guys are."

Debbie and Darlene nodded, their mouths hanging open. They didn't know anything about guys at all; neither of them had had a date yet. Lara wasn't even sure if *she* knew what she meant. Brittany had told her that guys noticed everything about a girl's appearance. They just weren't big on compliments.

"I bet Tim asks you out after dress rehearsal Wednesday night," Debbie said.

Darlene sighed. "You're so lucky."

"Tim is *so* cute," Debbie said. Her brown eyes glazed over, looking dreamy.

"He's a hunk," Darlene agreed. "And you're friends with Brittany Tate, too! I can't stand it."

"She's really nice," Lara said. "She might even introduce me to Kim Bishop and Jeremy Pratt."

"Wow," Darlene said reverently. She was deeply impressed by the River Heights High social scene.

"Never mind *them*," Debbie said. "Concentrate on Tim. I can't wait to hear what happens after dress rehearsal."

Lara hugged her books to her chest. She couldn't wait, either. Brittany had told her that dress rehearsal might be the night to make her big move.

Nikki dreaded dress rehearsal. As she waited for Tim to pick her up after dinner, she wondered what Friday night would be like if she was this nervous on Wednesday.

She and Tim were getting along, but that didn't mean much. They seldom saw each other alone these days. They'd been too busy with the play to do anything but go to school, rehearse, and sleep.

When Tim came to the door, his face was flushed with excitement. "I can't wait to get in costume and get up onstage," he said as he walked Nikki to the car.

"Me, too," she said weakly.

At a light, Tim reached over to pat her hand. "We haven't had much of a chance to talk the past few days," he said. "Why don't we go for something to eat after rehearsal? I promise I won't talk about the play," he added with a grin.

Nikki grinned back. "I'll hold you to that, Cooper."

The light turned green, and Tim put his hand back on the steering wheel. "I know we'll probably be exhausted, but it may be our last chance to be alone before opening night."

"I know. It sounds great, Tim." Nikki settled back into the seat. Happiness coursed through her. Tim wanted to be alone with her.

She didn't remember to be nervous again until they walked into the auditorium. Tim held the door for her and then strode in briskly. Nikki followed more slowly.

There was an electric feeling in the air as everyone rushed around, laughing and chattering excitedly. Girls helped one another with their hair, and Mrs. Burns went over lighting cues with Nick. Kevin Hoffman, already in costume, stood onstage, his mouth moving silently as he went over his lines.

Nikki hurried to keep up with Tim. Then she saw Lara wave to them from the stage, and she wanted to turn around again. Nikki had worn a white sweatshirt and her oldest jeans, knowing that she'd be changing into her costume right away, but Lara looked fabulous in a purple minidress.

Lara had gone to all that trouble when in five minutes she'd be made up as the middle-aged Mrs. Gibbs. Nikki felt a hot spurt of jealousy.

"Isn't it exciting?" Lara said. Her emerald eyes shone. "It's almost like opening night! I hope everything goes well."

"Well, you know what they say—the worse the dress rehearsal, the better the opening night," Tim said absently, taking in the other actors.

"Is that really true?" Lara said breathlessly, her eyes fastened on Tim. "You know all the theatrical superstitions, Tim."

Nikki's stomach lurched. She couldn't believe the sappy way Lara was looking at Tim.

Tim didn't seem to notice. "Well, I don't think I believe it," he said. "A bad dress rehearsal usually means a bad opening night, period."

"It must be great to have so much experience," Lara said, her voice like spun sugar.

"I guess. Well, we'd better get into costume," Tim said. "In another minute Mrs. Burns will be over here yelling at us to get a move on."

Nikki silently followed Tim and a still-chattering Lara backstage to the dressing rooms. In her head, she went over her opening lines for Act One. Actually, she wasn't too worried about Act One. It was Act Two that sent a shiver down her spine. In that act, Emily married George Gibbs, and then the action flashed back to the first time they realized they were in love. It was a tender and touching scene. She and Tim had to convey a delicate emotion without trying too hard. Nikki knew it would be the most difficult scene to pull off.

As she watched Lara put a hand on Tim's arm to ask him a question, Nikki wondered how she could possibly act as if she loved Tim when all she wanted to do was punch him in the nose.

Nikki hadn't been right to dread dress rehearsal. Her performance was okay in the first act, a little strained in the second, but in the third act, everything came together.

Emily was older in Act Three. She had died in childbirth, but she was allowed to return to life for one last, ordinary day. There was such simple beauty in the lines she spoke.

Near the end of the play, Emily asked the Stage Manager why people couldn't realize how beautiful life was every minute they lived it. Nikki felt something take her over as she delivered the speech. Her words rushed out into the darkened auditorium with grace and power. She didn't even see Kevin Hoffman, and she forgot about Mrs. Burns. She even forgot about Tim. She was Emily Webb crying out for life.

When the curtain came down and the cast clapped enthusiastically for themselves, Tim hurried toward her, grinning.

"You did it!" he said, hugging her. He held her at arm's length. "If you do that on opening night, you'll be a star."

"Thanks, Tim," Nikki said, her mouth suddenly dry. Her heart was beating very quickly. It seemed like ages since Tim had really kissed her, not just pecked her on the cheek.

Nikki realized how much she'd missed Tim's kisses, so soft and warm, telling her that he loved her in a way that words never could.

Tim leaned closer.

"Hey, you guys! Come on! Mrs. Burns wants the stage cleared." Lara Bennett poked her head around the curtain. Nikki could have cheerfully pushed her off the stage.

"Okay, Lara," Tim called. He winked at Nikki. "We'll continue this later," he whispered to her.

Nikki flew offstage to get changed. The rehearsal couldn't have ended on a better note. She climbed back into her jeans and sweatshirt and headed for the back of the auditorium.

Tim was waiting there with Lara. She was standing very close to him, laughing. Nikki noted how close they were standing, how Tim was laughing, too. He hardly ever laughed that way with her anymore, Nikki thought with a pang.

"You're sure you don't mind?" Lara asked Tim as Nikki came up.

"I'm sure, Lara," Tim said. He turned to Nikki. "Lara needs a ride home. Is that okay?"

"Fine," Nikki said brightly.

Tim turned back to Lara. "We'll drop you off first. Nikki and I are going out for a bite."

"Oh, are you really? I'm starving. I don't think I could go to sleep now, do you? I'm just so full of energy."

"Well . . ." Tim said. He glanced quickly at Nikki and gave her a helpless shrug.

Nikki couldn't believe it. Tim was going to let Lara horn in on their date! How *could* he?

"Why don't you come along?" Tim asked amiably. "We're going to the Loft."

"I'd love to. That sounds great." Lara

beamed as she glanced from Nikki to Tim. "Are you sure I'm not butting in?"

"Positive," Tim said. "Don't worry about it."

Fury and helplessness washed over Nikki. Was there really something going on between Lara and Tim? Tim would never sneak around behind her back, she knew. But he could have refused to let Lara tag along, and he didn't. In fact, Tim looked perfectly happy to have Lara join them. He seemed to have forgotten that he'd said they needed to be alone.

Nikki heard Mrs. Burns behind her. "Where's my Emily?"

Nikki turned. "Here, Mrs. Burns!"

"Nikki! Nikki dear, could you wait just a few minutes? I'd like a tiny word or two with you about Act Two."

"Sure, Mrs. Burns," Nikki answered. "I'll be right there." She turned to Tim and Lara. "Why don't you two go ahead?" she suggested icily. "I'm not sure how long this will take."

"Are you sure?" Lara asked, her face brightening.

"We'll wait," Tim said.

"I don't want you to," Nikki said. She gritted her teeth. "Mrs. Burns can take me home."

Their gazes held. Tim stared stonily at her. Nikki tried to keep her own gaze steady.

"If that's what you want," Tim said firmly.

"That's what I want," Nikki replied.

Tim shrugged. "Okay."

Nikki stood and watched Tim and Lara leave. She felt very cool and strong, but most of all, she felt very stupid.

10

The play started at eight on Friday night. Jeremy was supposed to pick Kim up by seven-thirty. At seven he was just finishing his last stack of dishes. Five minutes later he slammed out the door of the restaurant. The bus took forever, and it was seven thirty-three when he finally reached home.

Jeremy charged through the front door and up the stairs, unbuttoning his shirt as he ran. He splashed water on his face and hair and doused himself with cologne to cover the smell of grease. Then he climbed into his gray Italian suit and black shoes and the light blue dress shirt Kim loved. He stuck a tie in his pocket, grabbed his wallet and keys, and was behind the wheel of his mother's Lincoln Continental by seven forty-two.

Luckily Kim lived pretty close. He saw a curtain move in the living room as he pulled into the driveway. Jeremy hit the steering wheel in exasperation. She could run out by herself since they were so late, but, no, that wasn't Kim's style. He had to go up and ring the bell.

Jeremy bounced on his toes impatiently while he waited on the front steps. How long could it take Kim to get from the living room to the front door?

Kim's face was glacial when she swung open the door. "You're here," she said frostily.

Jeremy made the biggest effort of his life and turned on the charm. He took both of Kim's hands in his. "I'm really sorry, Kim. I'll make this up to you, I promise. You look so beautiful, too. Are you sure you want to go to a crowded auditorium?" he added meaningfully.

Kim's slight change in expression told him she was pleased. She smoothed the skirt of her ice blue dress. "Don't be silly," she said. "Of course we have to go. Did your mom's party run late?"

"My mom's party?" Jeremy completely blanked out. Kim was eyeing him suspiciously. Finally he remembered. "Right. It did run late." He took Kim's arm and led her down the walk. "She loves opening presents. She really drags it out."

"What did you get her?"

"A—a blouse, I think."

Kim was instantly interested. "Oh? Where did you get it? What was it like?"

"It was beige. I got it at the mall. Here, get in the car."

Kim was scowling when Jeremy came around and got in the driver's seat.

"I thought the Porsche would be fixed by now," she said. "This car looks like a hearse. I mean, it's fine for your parents, but—"

Jeremy tuned her out and concentrated on driving. After a while Kim fell silent. It was turning out to be one terrific date. He'd had a better time washing dishes and listening to Slim yell.

Brittany skidded into the auditorium at ten to eight. She'd taken her dress to work and changed at Slim and Shorty's, getting a good deal of razzing when she emerged from the tiny washroom.

"Oh, so that's what you look like," Slim had said.

Over the past week she'd gotten used to Slim's temper and Shorty's brusqueness. She hadn't gotten used to the uniform, the customers, or the dirty trays. And she hadn't gotten used to dodging Jeremy Pratt. The tension was going to drive her out of her mind. There he was now, sitting with Kim in the very back row. Kim's face looked like a thundercloud. Brittany waved gaily to them, then continued down the aisle. She saw Robin Fisher and Calvin Roth in the first row next to Lacey Dupree and Rick Stratton. She was glad to see that Nikki's friends had such good seats to watch her flop. Ben Newhouse and Emily Van Patten were in the second row right behind them. Ben was twisted around in his seat, talking to Karen Jacobs.

Finally Brittany spotted Samantha saving a seat for her in the fifth row. Brittany waved to her. She had just enough time to slip backstage and wish Nikki, Tim, and Lara good luck. She knew how much they would appreciate that.

Nikki was sitting in a chair with her eyes closed when Brittany found her backstage. Her face looked dead white. She was wearing a long skirt and old-fashioned middy blouse for the first act.

Brittany tapped her on the shoulder. Nikki opened her eyes, startled. "I just came to wish you good luck, Nikki."

Nikki winced. "Thanks."

"There's a packed house out there," Brittany said cheerfully. "Everyone's really excited about this play. I just spoke to Tim and

Lara, and they're ready to go. They didn't seem too nervous, but then, they're pros, pretty much."

Nikki's face got even paler. She closed her eyes again. "See you later, Brittany."

"Sure." Brittany moved away, feeling pleased. She might have another story on her hands for the *Record*. How the star of the show passed out before her performance. Wouldn't that be a terrific scoop!

Lacey and Robin bounded up to Nikki soon after Brittany left.

"You look great, Nikki," Robin said.

"We'll be out there cheering you on," Lacey added cheerfully. "Good luck."

Nikki smiled ruefully. "Don't say that, okay?"

"Say what?" Robin asked. "Good luck?"

Nikki put her hands over her ears. "It's bad luck to say good luck to an actor before a performance. You're supposed to say 'break a leg.'" She sighed. "Brittany Tate already jinxed me." She stuck out a hand. "Feel this."

"Freezing," Lacey said.

Nikki clutched her stomach. "And I feel sick. I'm dizzy, too." She raised her head and looked at her best friends hopefully. "Do you think I'm getting the flu?"

"No chance," Robin said flatly.

"It's stage fright," Lacey said. "You'll be fine once the curtain goes up."

"We'd better get back, Lacey," Robin said. "Break a leg, Nik."

"Break a leg," Lacey repeated cheerfully, following Robin out the door.

Nikki closed her eyes and tried a breathing exercise Mrs. Burns had taught her to relax. It didn't work.

When she opened her eyes again, Tim was standing in front of her. They'd been avoiding each other since dress rehearsal, and she was surprised to see him. He looked worried, and Nikki felt instantly defensive.

"Break a leg," Tim said. He leaned over and kissed her lightly. His lips felt very warm against her cold cheek.

Nikki nodded.

Then Lara appeared behind Tim, looking plump in her old-fashioned dress padded at the hips for her role as Mrs. Gibbs. "Come on, Tim. Mrs. Burns called places."

Lara and Tim would make their entrances from stage right, Nikki from stage left. "Okay," Tim said. Lara pulled at his arm, and the two of them walked off together.

Nikki rose slowly, picked up the schoolbook she would carry in the first scene, and made her way to the wings. She could hear the murmur of the audience. She imagined her parents, Lacey and Rick, and Robin and

Cal, all of them wishing her well. Then there was Brittany Tate, waiting to see her fail. . . .

The curtain rose and there was polite applause. Kevin Hoffman walked out, a pipe in his mouth, and people clapped again. He began positioning the chairs and benches that would serve as the set.

Nikki crossed her fingers, just in case. She'd never felt so terrified in her life. She couldn't see the audience, but she could hear them rustling in their seats.

Tim and Lara were waiting in the wings across the stage. Were they standing very close in the darkness? Were their fingers touching?

She heard the opening lines of the play. She knew them by heart, almost as well as her own first line. Her first line was—

Panic shot through Nikki so violently that she was lucky she didn't scream. *She'd forgotten her first line!* Her mind was a complete blank.

Nikki woke slowly and reluctantly the next morning. For an instant she didn't know why she was so unwilling to face the new day.

Then she remembered opening night.

Nikki burrowed under the covers and moaned.

She'd remembered her lines, after all. And

she hadn't missed a cue. She'd hit her mark every time.

But her performance had been *awful.* She'd been terrible in the first act, dismal in the second, and had only pulled it together— almost—in the third. The whole night had been a nightmare.

Nikki burrowed deeper beneath the covers, as though every person in River Heights was standing in her sunny bedroom, staring down at her. She was mortified.

Then Nikki heard her phone ringing on the nightstand. Briefly, she considered not answering it, but decided she couldn't be a flop *and* a coward.

She crawled out from under the quilt and picked up the receiver gingerly. "Hello?"

"I went to see you backstage last night, but you probably don't remember," Robin said.

Nikki leaned back against the headboard. "Since when did you learn to be so tactful?"

"Nik, what can I say? You weren't as good as you wanted to be, as you *could* have been, but you weren't as awful as you think you were. I think you did really well in the third act."

"Really?" Nikki said hopefully.

"Really. And you'll be even better tonight. Did you practice that relaxation exercise before you went on?"

"I tried to," Nikki said. "But then Brittany Tate showed up."

"We should hang a bell around that girl's neck," Robin grumbled. "Hey. Did you see Tim after the play?"

"Just for a second," Nikki said with a sigh. "He didn't look very happy. My parents brought me right home."

"Well, you and Tim can work things out at the cast party tonight. Lacey and I'll come over this afternoon and give you a pep talk, okay?"

"That'll be great, Robin. Thanks."

They said goodbye, and Nikki hung up. The phone rang again immediately. She knew it would be Lacey, and it was.

"It's not that bad," Lacey said immediately. "I mean, it's not like he singled you out or anything. And who reads the paper on Saturday morning, anyway?"

Nikki gulped. "What are you talking about?" she asked hoarsely.

There was a long pause. "Oh," Lacey said in a small voice. "You haven't seen the review yet?"

"Review? What review?" Then realization dawned on Nikki. The theater critic must have come the night before. "Is it awful?" she asked.

"No, no." Lacey rushed to reassure her. "It's not bad at all."

Lacey was a terrible liar. "I'll call you back," Nikki said, and hung up. She threw on her robe and raced downstairs to the kitchen, where her parents were sitting with their coffee. The morning paper was on the kitchen table. They tried to smile at her brightly.

"Good morning, honey," her mother said.

"Morning, pumpkin," her father said.

Nikki groaned. "It must be really bad," she said.

"Oh, no," her mother said. "It's not *really* bad, dear."

Nikki reached for the paper. Her fingers riffled the pages until she found the entertainment section. She sank into a kitchen chair to read the review.

Her parents waited silently. She could feel their apprehension as she read the whole thing, carefully and slowly. Finally she looked up.

Her mother was frowning. "It's not too awful, is it?"

Her father patted Nikki's shoulder. "Opening night jitters," he said. "Maybe this guy will come back and review another performance. What does he know, anyway?"

"He went to the Yale School of Drama," Nikki said numbly.

"See?" her father said heartily. He put his hands in his pockets and leaned back in his chair. "A frustrated actor, I'll bet. You were great, pumpkin."

"No, I wasn't, Daddy," Nikki said. "The critic was right. There *was* no romantic tension between me and Tim. The second act *did* lack warmth. And I *did* give a 'barely adequate' performance." She picked up the paper again. "I thought everyone else did pretty well, but he seemed to think the whole production was mediocre, except for one 'riveting performance,'" Nikki said flatly. She read from the paper. "'Lara Bennett, in the role of Mrs. Gibbs, gives a riveting performance. She shows genuine promise as an actress.'"

"Well," Mr. Masters said, unable to come up with anything more.

"But, Daddy, this part is the worst. 'Tim Cooper, in the role of George Gibbs, struggles manfully to inject some romance into his scenes with Emily Webb. But he sinks under the weight of Nikki Masters's leaden performance.'"

Nikki put her head down and banged it lightly on the table. "I just want to die," she said. "What am I going to do now?"

Mrs. Masters sat down next to her. She smoothed Nikki's blond hair off her face and took her chin in her hand. "You're going to get back up on that stage tonight and do it all over again," she said.

11

On Saturday Brittany's first shift was over at six. She had forty-five minutes to get home and eat before rushing back to Slim and Shorty's in time for the dinner hour.

The really tricky part was getting her coat. She had to hang it by the back door, and every day she had to wait around until Jeremy was gone before getting it. It helped that he was out the door like a flash at the end of his shift. She always had to add up her tickets and give them to Shorty.

Brittany listened carefully at the partition, but she didn't hear the sound of running water. She peeked around. No one was at the sink.

Brittany made a beeline for her coat. She

threw it over her shoulders, yanked open the back door, and stepped out into the cold night air. She was safe. Now she wouldn't have to worry about Jeremy Pratt for the rest of the night.

She was just congratulating herself on that fact when she turned the corner and ran right into him.

Brittany screamed and put a hand to her throat. "You scared me half to death, Jeremy Pratt!"

Jeremy looked down at the ground and jammed his hands in his pockets.

"What are you doing here?" Brittany demanded. "I just came by for a bite, and—"

"Get off it, Brittany. I know you're lying—your nose is twitching." As Brittany's hand flew to her nose, Jeremy added casually, "I was just coming in for some dinner—"

"Get real, Pratt," Brittany said hotly. "I've seen you back there in your ugly rubber gloves—"

"And you're wearing that grungy uniform under your coat," Jeremy shot back.

Brittany's eyes blazed. "You mean you *knew* I was working here?"

Jeremy nodded. "And you knew—"

Brittany nodded.

They stared at each other furiously. Then they both burst out laughing.

"I'll make you a deal," Jeremy said. "If you don't say anything, I won't say anything."

Could she trust Jeremy Pratt? Brittany knew she really didn't have a choice. She held out her hand. "Deal," she said.

Jeremy frowned. "So why are *you* working here?" he asked.

"For the *Record,*" Brittany said promptly, tossing her head. "I'm writing an article about the 'other side' of River Heights."

"Oh," Jeremy said. "I'm here for a social studies project. Extra credit. 'Minimum Wage Workers and Their Concerns,'" he added.

They looked at each other again. A smile began to tug at the corners of Brittany's lips. Jeremy raised one eyebrow.

"Okay, why are you *really* here?" he asked.

Brittany sighed. "Why do you think? I need the money to pay my membership dues at the club."

"You told me you had it covered."

Brittany shrugged. "I *do,* now that I'm working at Slim and Shorty's. What about you?" she asked. "That's a much bigger mystery."

Jeremy looked at her as though he was deciding whether or not to trust her. "It's a

long story," he said. "And I h
dinner break."

"You're doing a double shift?
can't stand eating the gross food

Jeremy shrugged. "Well, if you
can come over to my house for dinner.
parents are out, but my mom left me some
kind of casserole. My mother lent me her car,
too."

Dinner with Jeremy Pratt? Once, Brittany
would have preferred to eat gerbil food, but
he seemed almost human now. Besides, she
was dying to know why he was working as a
dishwasher. "Okay," she agreed. "Let's go."

Kim picked at her dinner and refused her
parents' offer to take her to the movies with
them. That'd be the day, when she'd go out
with her parents on a Saturday night!

She sat in her room for a while, trying to
watch TV, but all she could think about was
Jeremy. Was his uncle really visiting from
out of town? And if he was, why couldn't
Jeremy manage to get away for a few hours?
Why did she have to sit all alone in her room
on a Saturday night?

She could have called Samantha, but she
couldn't remember if Samantha had a date or
not. Anyway, she wouldn't be able to stand
hearing the honeyed sympathy drip from

ents wouldn't be crazy about her borrowing the car without asking, but she'd probably be back before they were.

Jeremy had never seen her mother's navy blue Honda. He'd never guess it was Kim if he saw the car outside his house or behind him on the road.

Kim hadn't figured out what she'd do if she caught Jeremy cheating on her. The thing was to catch him first.

Nikki sat back while Sasha pinned the big pink bow in her hair. It was the final touch to transform her into Emily Webb once again. She felt much calmer than she had the night before, thanks to her friends.

Robin and Lacey had done a pretty good job of cheering her up that afternoon. Her parents had been great, too. When Nikki reached the auditorium that night, it seemed as though every member of the cast and crew had come over and told her the review was unfair. It was nice to know that so many people were pulling for her. The only one who seemed to want her to fail, Nikki realized, was herself.

She'd done some hard thinking that day. Somewhere along the way she must have decided that, if she let Tim and the other actors shine, she wouldn't be noticed, wouldn't be singled out. The only trouble was, no matter what she did, she would get noticed. She was playing the female lead! Of course she'd get a lot of attention!

Nikki couldn't believe she'd been so stupid. She'd been afraid to give a really strong performance! Afraid it would bring her too much attention.

She just hoped it wasn't too late to do a good job. Everyone was telling her she'd do just great.

Everyone but Tim. Nikki didn't blame him. He had been a victim of her lousy performance, hadn't he? She'd spoiled his big dream. Of course he hated her now.

The cast party that night would be torture. Nikki didn't know how she'd get through it. Her black velvet dress was hanging up in a bag in the dressing room, where the girls would all change after the show. Her suede pumps and pearls and the new earrings Robin had made her buy were there, too. Nikki wanted only to run home after the performance and go straight to bed. Just thinking about Tim brought tears to her eyes.

Nikki closed her eyes. She was determined to become Emily Webb. This time it was a lot easier. Because the last person on earth she wanted to be right then was Nikki Masters.

After five minutes of sitting outside the huge Pratt house, Kim began to feel silly. She squirmed impatiently in the driver's seat. There were lights on downstairs, and the long black Lincoln Continental was in the driveway. The Pratts were probably all inside, having a family party. Kim was spending Saturday night sitting in a cold car on a dark street doing nothing—and she'd thought watching TV in her room was pathetic!

Just as she was about to give up and turn the key in the ignition, the front door opened. Kim almost dived under the front seat when she saw Jeremy come out. What if he saw her?

When she got the courage to look again, she tensed with fury. He was with a *girl!* Kim couldn't see her very well. She was on the other side of Jeremy as they walked to the car, but it was a girl, all right. She was wearing a dark coat and ugly white shoes. At least she had no fashion sense.

So Jeremy had lied! Kim strained her eyes to peer through the blackness. It was a moonless night, and it was impossible to see details. Jeremy started the car and backed out of the driveway. Kim ducked down again until she heard the car go by. Then she grimly started the engine.

Where were they headed? she wondered bitterly. Le Saint-Tropez? Café Chow, where the Westmoor students hung out? Jeremy wouldn't take his date to the Loft or Pizza Palace—there'd be too much danger of running into someone he knew. Or running into Kim herself.

Jeremy was certainly not headed anywhere Kim knew, she thought as she followed him down unfamiliar streets. They were heading toward the river. Not where they swam in summer or near the country club, but toward the part of the riverfront where *nobody* went. Jeremy sure didn't have to worry about being recognized out there.

Kim almost fainted when Jeremy pulled into a dilapidated shack called Slim and Shorty's Good Eats Cafe. A pink neon sign blinked at her. What was going on, anyway?

She pulled up close to the curb in front of the entrance to the rutted parking lot. Then she leaned toward the windshield and waited for her two-timing jerk of a boyfriend to get out of his mom's car. Both doors opened. Jeremy got out on one side. Kim craned her neck for a view of Jeremy's date. The windshield fogged and she wiped it with her sleeve impatiently. Now she saw Jeremy's companion clearly. It was Brittany Tate! Her *best friend.*

The rage that had been simmering inside Kim for days boiled over. Kim felt as though she could fly across the parking lot and pound the two of them into smithereens.

No wonder Brittany had been so evasive. No wonder Jeremy had lied. No wonder they had driven all the way across town to this awful little place. Kim was shocked, even considering the circumstances, that either of them would go into such a dump.

But what if it wasn't a dump? she thought suddenly. What if it was the new cool place to go? Kim closed her eyes in pain. Of course! It was the new diner craze—meat loaf and pot roast, Mom's apple pie. The place was probably hopping with Westmoor students. Then on Monday Brittany would come in bragging about the new hot spot she'd found. Maybe Jeremy would be with her. Maybe they'd decide that the time for secrecy was over. Kim would be humiliated in front of the entire school!

Kim felt like screaming. She'd lost Jeremy already. Her best friend had stolen him away! All that sniping between Brittany and Jeremy was just an act. They didn't hate each other at all. Kim would never be able to hold her head up at River Heights High again. It was enough to make her cry— almost. Nobody, she told herself fiercely, made Kim Bishop cry.

She lifted her chin and pressed her lips together in a thin line. She wouldn't let them get away with it. She'd sit there, and she'd wait. Let them have their trendy dinner, let them laugh at her behind her back. She'd be waiting. She'd humiliate them, and then she'd tell the whole school about it first thing on Monday.

Kim smiled a small, chilling smile. By Monday afternoon, Jeremy Pratt and Brittany Tate would be history.

 **12**

After the play Robin, Calvin, Lacey, and Rick crowded around Nikki backstage. Lacey thrust a bouquet of yellow tea roses into Nikki's hand.

"You were wonderful," she said. Rick nodded behind her and gave Nikki the thumbs-up sign. "It was worth seeing a second time."

"Terrific!" Robin said. Her rhinestone earrings danced with her enthusiasm. "You really seemed more confident tonight." Beside her, Calvin nodded in agreement.

"Thanks, guys," Nikki said as she sniffed her roses. "I know I still didn't do my best." She looked up and smiled. "But at least I did a lot better. I am impressed," she added mischievously, "that you all came again!"

They all laughed. Calvin and Rick wandered off to congratulate Kevin Hoffman.

"So, did Tim say anything to you tonight?" Robin asked.

"I noticed he held your hand during the curtain call," Lacey said.

Nikki shrugged. "He dropped it as soon as the curtain came down."

"Maybe you'll make up at the cast party," Lacey said encouragingly.

"I hope so," Nikki said. "I think we just need some time alone. But I have to take a bunch of people in my car to the party."

"That's okay," Robin said, her eyes sparkling. "Just don't take them *home.*"

Nikki laughed. "Right. Listen, I'd better go and change."

"Can I say good luck now?" Lacey asked teasingly.

Nikki nodded energetically. "You bet. Now I need all the luck I can get."

Nikki said goodbye and made her way to the dressing room to change.

Lara was flushed and chattering, obviously excited about the party ahead. She was wearing another new dress, a sea green creation that enhanced the color of her eyes. Nikki slipped into her black velvet dress, feeling very drab.

Several kids, including Tim, piled into

Nikki's car for the short ride to Mrs. Burns's house.

"I was terrific, wasn't I?" said Kevin Hoffman, squeezing into the back seat next to Sasha Lopez.

Everyone laughed at the face Sasha made. Then Lara said seriously, "I think Tim did even better tonight than last night."

Tim smiled and said, "Thanks."

"You were really good, too, Lara," Martin Salko said.

"Did you see in Act Two when Cheryl almost forgot her lines?" Kevin asked. "I poked her from behind with my pipe."

They all laughed again, their spirits high. Tim and Nikki were silent, but nobody noticed. There was too much noise and laughter in the car.

Nikki pulled into the driveway of Mrs. Burns's small Tudor house. It was ablaze with lights when they drove up. Soft music floated out through the trees, and tiny pink lights twinkled in the shrubs.

"Wow," Lara said. "It's soooo romantic."

Nikki opened the car door with a heavy heart. She had a feeling that romance was the last thing she'd find that night. Would Lara be any luckier?

Shivering, Kim turned off the ignition. She couldn't run the heater anymore; she was running low on gas. She couldn't run the radio anymore, either; she didn't want to drain the battery. That was all she needed, to deliver her stinging speech, flounce to her car, and not be able to peel out! She'd just have to sit and freeze.

What could Jeremy and Brittany be doing in there? she wondered for the thousandth time. It was ten-thirty! They must have finished dinner hours ago. They were obviously having a fabulous time.

Kim pounded a frantic drumbeat against the dashboard with her fingertips. She was freezing, and she'd never been so bored in her life. As a rule, she didn't like to spend much time alone. Over the last couple of hours, she'd mentally cataloged her wardrobe, rearranged her makeup drawer, and planned her English paper. Jeremy and Brittany were still eating. She hoped Brittany would put on twenty pounds just from dinner.

Kim stretched her cramped legs. She'd gone for a short walk earlier, but she didn't dare go far for fear she'd miss them. Besides, the neighborhood was definitely creepy. She'd done some quick ballet exercises holding on to the hood, but a man walking by had looked at her as if she was crazy. She'd jumped back in the car fast and locked the door.

With every minute that ticked by, Kim's resentment grew. She couldn't wait to see Brittany's face when she told her that she wouldn't be sponsoring her for the country club. And she was dying to see Jeremy's reaction when she told him he was a low-down, cowardly weasel—and didn't know how to kiss, either.

She would say all that, and more. First, though, Jeremy and Brittany had to leave the restaurant. There was no way Kim could make a scene like that in public. Kim stared at the door of the restaurant until her eyes burned. What were they *doing* in there?

Samantha slammed her French book shut. So she was practically flunking French—did that mean she had to study on a Saturday night? She had a whole long, boring Sunday to hit the books.

She took an apple out of the bowl on the kitchen table. At least she'd heard some good news on Friday. Her French teacher, that old bag Madame Duval, had broken her hip. Samantha did feel terrible about the accident. Madame would be laid up for months.

Maybe she'd enjoy her time off and not have to pound irregular verb tenses into bored teenage heads.

Samantha bit into the apple thoughtfully. There probably wouldn't be a Monday morning quiz. Some dumb substitute teacher would go over the lesson in a droning voice, and he wouldn't pick on Samantha the way Madame did, because he couldn't know she never did her homework. Things were looking up.

Sort of. Samantha lost interest in the apple and tossed it into the garbage. It was still a dateless Saturday night. It was her own fault. She'd turned down several dates. She'd already run through all of the halfway interesting unattached boys at River Heights High, and she was bored, bored, bored.

What she needed was a vanilla caramel swirl ice-cream sundae with hot fudge. Maybe even whipped cream. The works.

She couldn't go to any of the River Heights High hangouts, though. What if she ran into someone? She'd die if anyone caught her pigging out by herself on a Saturday night.

There was that terrific ice-cream store just a half-mile away where her parents sometimes went after a movie. Perfect.

Slipping into her fleece-lined denim jacket, Samantha went out to her mom's car. It was a five-minute drive, and her mouth was watering when she arrived, but she waited to make sure the store was empty except for a gray-haired couple near the back eating ice-cream cones. She didn't want to take any chances.

Samantha raced into the store. "A vanilla caramel swirl sundae with hot fudge to go," she told the server quickly.

"Right." He turned slowly, his scoop poised in the air, and blinked at her. "What did you say? Vanilla fudge?"

"Vanilla caramel swirl," Samantha repeated impatiently. She heard the bell tinkle at the front door. Someone else came in and stood behind her.

"And what else?" The server stood with the ice cream in a plastic container.

"Hot fudge," Samantha said sweetly, trying not to snap at him.

"Whipped cream?"

Samantha hesitated.

"Oh, go ahead," a deep voice said behind her. "What's a sundae without whipped cream?"

A deep voice with a hint of humor in it. This might be interesting. Samantha turned around and almost fainted dead away.

He was young. He was gorgeous. He had dark hair and brown eyes that twinkled at her. He was slim, but she suspected there were plenty of muscles beneath that jacket.

"Whipped cream," Samantha said over her shoulder to the server. She smiled her most flirtatious smile at the stranger. "Absolutely. I couldn't live without it."

"Ah, a southern lady," the guy said, smiling back.

"Transplanted," Samantha said as she paid for her sundae. "I live in River Heights now."

"Strawberry cone," the stranger told the server. "I'm studying at Westmoor," he added to Samantha.

She nodded, still smiling, while her mind worked frantically. Her sundae was in a plastic take-out container. But if he stayed there to eat his cone, should she stay, too? Would he suggest it? Would it look weird if she kept standing there with her ice cream melting, making conversation? She just couldn't let this hunk get away.

"What are you studying?" she asked.

"French. I'm in the graduate program."

"Really? What a coincidence! I was just studying *my* French tonight. I came out for a break." Samantha gestured to her ice cream.

The stranger paid for his cone. "I'm Marc LeBlanc," he said.

"Samantha Daley," she said. She pressed her lips together to show her dimples. "This must be my lucky day."

He took a lick of his cone and grinned. "Oh, yes? Why?"

"Because I'm flunking French," she said with a naughty lift of her eyebrows. "And I just met a smart graduate student." She wished he would ask her to sit down, but Marc merely leaned against the counter, licking his cone, grinning at her.

"Ah. But how do you know I'm smart?"

"Oh, that's one of my secrets," Samantha said in her most flirtatious manner. Nobody could flirt as well as she could. Not even Brittany. Samantha had been flirting since she was in diapers. "I can't reveal it yet. I can't tell just anyone, you know."

Marc's smile grew broader. "Who's your French teacher?" he asked.

"My what?"

"Your French teacher."

"Oh. Madame Duval."

Marc frowned. "Duval. I don't think I know her."

Oh, no! He thought she went to Westmoor! Samantha considered what to do as her ice cream slowly dripped through the container and down her hand. She *could* let him think she was a college student. That was what Brittany would do, but that could backfire too easily. She'd just have to tell him the truth and hope it wouldn't make a difference. If she charmed him enough, it wouldn't.

"I don't go to Westmoor," Samantha said in her huskiest voice. "I go to River Heights High." She shrugged a bit as if to say, Now, isn't that ridiculous?

Marc backed up a step. "Well, well," he

said heartily. "What do you know? I'll be substitute teaching there on Monday."

"Really?" Samantha said with fake enthusiasm. Marc seemed a little put off. Then a thought occurred to her. "You must be replacing Madame Duval! You'll be my teacher!"

Marc nodded. "Great!" he said cheerfully. "I should be able to help you with your French, then."

Samantha inched a little closer. "I'm looking forward to it."

Marc took another lick of his cone. "Well, it was great meeting you, uh—"

"Samantha."

"Samantha. I'll see you on Monday, I guess."

He was gone in a flash. Dreamily, Samantha sat down at one of the tiny wrought-iron tables. Marc LeBlanc might not want to get involved with a student, but she could change his mind. Besides, he wouldn't be substitute teaching forever.

Samantha pushed her sundae away. Let it melt, she thought. She didn't need ice cream anymore. Samantha smiled her trademark catlike smile. Things were definitely looking up.

Mrs. Burns had insisted that the party begin with music that she chose. The kids could play the Dead Beats later, if they wanted, but she wanted to ease into the evening with something a little mellower.

Everyone had groaned good-naturedly, but Mrs. Burns had been great about letting them have their party at her house and the Gershwin and Cole Porter tunes were actually fun to dance to. Everyone crowded onto the living room floor, enjoying the music. Mrs. Burns beamed at them from the doorway to the den.

Nikki refused all offers to dance. She sat by the fireplace, telling everyone she was a little tired from the show, but really she was waiting for Tim to ask her. He wasn't dancing, either. He was sitting as far away from her as he could, in a big red armchair by the door.

Then someone called, "Let's see George and Emily dance!"

"Yeah! Come on, George!"

"Get out there, Emily!"

"Let's see some romantic tension!" Kevin Hoffman teased in a loud voice. Everyone hooted with laughter. Nikki could have punched him.

She found herself dragged to the center of the dance floor, and then she was facing Tim. He didn't look at her, but only stiffly held out his arms. She walked into them. Mrs. Burns moved the needle and started to play "Some-one to Watch Over Me."

Tim held Nikki as though she might break. His fingers barely grazed hers. The touch of his hand on her back was so light she could barely feel it. Nikki spun around and around while the rest of the cast applauded. Tears stung her eyes.

Finally everyone else grabbed a partner and began to dance. The pressure was off.

"I'm sorry, Tim," Nikki said into his shoulder.

He pulled back a bit and frowned. "What?"

"I said I'm sorry you had to dance with me. I know you're mad."

"It's okay," he said. He drew her closer to him again. Nikki wished it was because he wanted to hold her. But she had a feeling it was because he didn't want to meet her eyes.

"Tim, I think we need to talk," Nikki said softly. "You thought so, too, a few days ago. That's why I was so upset when you let Lara butt in on our date the other night."

Tim's body went stiff. "What was I supposed to do, Nikki?"

"I don't want to argue about it now," Nikki said, pulling back so she could see his face. "Can't we just start all over again? I know you're angry because I messed up your performance on opening night, but——"

Tim's gray eyes were stormy. "I don't believe you," he said. "What kind of egotistical jerk do you think I am? I don't hate you for giving a bad performance, Nikki. You could forget all your lines and run off the stage and I'd still love you."

I'd still love you. Nikki felt more hopeful.

"But what's hard to forgive," Tim went on in a hard voice, "is that you don't trust me. You let yourself get all upset over Lara, and you let *that* ruin your performance. Actors can't hide from each other onstage, Nikki. I saw that mistrust in your eyes—and the audience sensed it, too." Tim's hand tightened on hers. "The fact that you'd let that happen, let it happen to *us* as well as the rest of the cast—well, that I just don't understand."

Tim broke away from Nikki. "I thought we trusted each other."

He turned quickly and walked off, leaving Nikki in the middle of the dance floor. All alone among the crowd of couples dancing cheek to cheek.

13

Kim squinted at her watch. Eleven o'clock! Jeremy and Brittany had been in Slim and Shorty's Good Eats Cafe for four hours. There were only a few cars left in the parking lot. She'd had it. She didn't care if she made a scene in a public place. She was going in.

Kim shouldered open the car door and slammed it shut with her heel. Then she marched across the parking lot. Mud splashed on her jeans, but she didn't care.

She pushed open the creaking door of the restaurant. With a rapidly beating heart, she scanned the tables. A tired-looking couple stared back, a baby asleep in a child-seat next to them. One lone burly man gave her the once-over, but there was no Jeremy or

Brittany. As a matter of fact the place looked as seedy inside as it did outside. This was the new River Heights hot spot?

Kim blinked in surprise. Where had they gone? Had they seen her follow them? Had they escaped by the back door? Were they at the Loft right now, laughing at her?

A new, hot spurt of rage filled her. Kim clenched her fists. Then she heard Brittany's distinctive laugh. But it was coming from behind the swinging doors. Kim frowned. She'd figured that the doors led to the kitchen, but maybe there was another dining room in the place.

Her shoulders squared, her chin high, Kim pushed through the swinging doors.

Brittany was leaning against the huge steel refrigerator, talking to some dumpy, disgusting man in an apron. She didn't even look up, and she was wearing a *waitress's* uniform!

Kim couldn't believe it. Then Jeremy walked out from behind a partition with an armload of plates. Kim was astonished to see that her so-called boyfriend was wearing an absolutely filthy apron.

Things started happening all at once. Jeremy's eyes met Kim's. He gasped, and the load of plates flew out of his arms and fell to the floor with a crash.

Brittany looked shocked, then started to laugh. The pudgy man swung into action. "You're paying for those plates, kid!" he shouted at Jeremy. Then he turned to Brittany. "What are you doing, hanging around back here while your customers are wandering all over the place? You—"

"Relax, Slim," Brittany said, grinning at the shock on Kim's face. "She isn't a customer."

Kim stepped forward regally. "My name is Kim Bishop. I'm Jeremy's girlfriend."

Slim looked baffled. "Jeremy? Who's Jeremy?"

"The kid," Brittany said helpfully.

Jeremy stepped gingerly around the plates and came over to Kim. "How did you find me?" he asked hoarsely.

"I followed you," Kim admitted. But she would never, ever admit she'd thought he was dating Brittany behind her back.

Brittany's eyes gleamed. "You must have been pretty surprised when you saw us together."

Kim shrugged. "I figured there had to be some logical explanation," she said.

"Mmmm," Brittany said meaningfully. "So you've been sitting in the parking lot for hours, waiting for us to come out, right?"

Kim ignored her and turned to Jeremy. "Can we talk?"

"Uh, sure," he said quickly, starting to untie his apron.

Slim threw his hands in the air. *"Sure? Don't I see a bunch of plates lying smashed on the floor, kid? Are they going to get up by themselves?"*

"Calm down, Slim," Brittany said. She actually put her hand on the man's greasy shoulder. "I'll clean them up."

This had to be the limit. Brittany was doing Jeremy a favor?

"Go ahead, kid," Brittany said to Jeremy with a wink. She smiled at Kim almost as if she was enjoying the situation. "You two need to talk."

"So what exactly do you *do* here?" Kim asked, leaning against the fence at the back of the parking lot. She shivered against the cold wind blowing up from the river.

Jeremy looked at the sky. "I'm a dishwasher."

"A *dishwasher!* You've got to be kidding!" Kim had never felt so revolted in her life. "And what is Brittany doing here?" she asked suspiciously.

"She's a waitress," Jeremy said simply.

"So did you two hatch this scheme together, or what? I mean, why here?" Kim shuddered. "This place is disgusting, Jeremy."

Jeremy shrugged. "I thought it was gross,

too, at first. Well, I mean, it *is* pretty gross. But you get used to it, I guess.''

"You're not answering my question," Kim pointed out.

"I didn't know Brittany was working here when I got the job," Jeremy told her. "Then when I found out, I didn't want her to know I was washing dishes here. We managed to avoid each other for a couple days, but we finally bumped into each other earlier tonight. We have a deal—I don't tell anyone, she doesn't tell anyone."

Jeremy looked straight at her, and Kim knew why. He wanted her to keep her mouth shut. Well, she might, and she might not. There was no need to make a decision so quickly. Especially since Jeremy seemed more worried about people finding out he was a dishwasher than he was about Kim being furious at him.

"But why?" she asked again.

Jeremy shrugged again. "Money, why else? Brittany had to earn her membership dues for the club."

"I see." Kim had never thought about how Brittany was going to get the money. She smiled slowly. This was great. This was terrific. She finally had something on Brittany, just in case she ever needed it. No wonder Brittany had been so nice back there in the kitchen! Imagine offering to clean up someone else's mess!

Kim felt so happy she wanted to dance across the parking lot. So Jeremy and Brittany weren't making a fool of her. In fact, the tables had turned completely.

She couldn't let Jeremy know how relieved she was. He still wasn't off the hook. So he was spending his time with a sinkful of dirty dishes instead of another girl. He'd still lied to her.

"What about you, Jeremy?" she asked. "Why did *you* get a job here?"

He sighed and leaned against the fence next to her. "It all started with the Porsche," he said, running a hand over his eyes. "It's going to cost a mint to fix the transmission, and my old man finally put his foot down. I couldn't do without wheels, Kim. Especially not since we started going out. You were *made* for that car, Kim."

Well, at least he got that right, Kim thought smugly.

"So I was desperate," Jeremy continued glumly. "And then I did a stupid thing." He sneaked a quick glance at Kim. "And I, uh, got into this big poker game at the club."

"You gambled?" Kim asked, shocked. "That was pretty stupid."

Jeremy didn't take offense. "You're not

kidding. Anyway, these prep school guys I was playing with were pretty high rollers. And they were rough, too. Before I knew it, I was in over my head, and they wanted their money the next day. When I told them they'd have to wait, they didn't like it too much. Things almost got out of hand.''

"You said you got that bruise from a door!" Kim exclaimed.

Jeremy nodded. "Yeah, well, sorry about that. It's just that Chip made this, uh, suggestion that I couldn't go for.''

"What suggestion?" Kim frowned. "Did he want something for collateral?''

"Sort of.'' Jeremy looked away again.

"Come on, Jeremy," Kim said. "You've told me this much. Tell me the rest.''

"He wanted you," Jeremy mumbled.

"What? *Me?* That's disgusting!''

"He wanted a date with you," Jeremy went on. "And I said no. I mean, I would have said no to anybody, Kim. But that guy Chip—just the thought of him being alone with you for one second drove me crazy.''

Unexpectedly, Kim felt touched. "You mean you got beaten up for me?" she asked.

"Well, I got away with just a punch or two, but they did tear my favorite shirt," Jeremy added.

Delicately, Kim touched the place where the bruise just barely showed now. "That was really brave, Jeremy. I can't believe you did that for me."

He met her gaze. "Of course I'd do that for you. You're my girlfriend. That is, I thought you were."

Kim smiled. She couldn't help it. "I'm still your girl," she said softly.

"Even without a Porsche?"

"Of course." Kim looked insulted. Then she hesitated. "When will it be fixed?"

Jeremy sighed. "Who knows? I'd use my salary here for it, but I have to hand the cash over to those goons tomorrow or I'll be dead meat."

Kim thought fast. She just might be able to salvage this whole fiasco. It would mean cutting into her clothing allowance. But Jeremy *had* almost gotten beaten to a pulp for her. She couldn't stand the idea of her boyfriend working at this disgusting grease joint every night. They'd never be able to go out and be seen together! And what if somebody else found out? Jeremy's social status —and her own—would drop to zero.

"I'll lend you the money," she said impulsively.

Jeremy shook his head. "Thanks, but I couldn't—"

"Yes, you could," Kim said briskly. "I have the cash, so why not? You'd have to pay me back, of course, but you'll get those

creeps off your back. It's the least I can do,"
she said, looking at him earnestly, "after you
defended my honor and everything, I mean."

"Well—"

"And you can quit this stupid job. I'm sure
you were a horrible dishwasher anyway."

"Actually," Jeremy said, frowning, "I was
a terrific dishwasher."

Kim let out a peal of laughter. "I'd better
get you out of here, Jeremy," she said. "The
soapsuds have gotten to your brain. I don't
want you changing on me."

"No way," he said, shaking his head.

"Glad to hear it," Kim murmured. "I kind
of liked the old Jeremy Pratt."

The invitation in her voice was impossible
to resist. Jeremy leaned over and kissed her.

"Come on," Kim said huskily when they
broke apart. "I can't wait to see Brittany's
face when you walk in there and quit."

"Yeah," Jeremy said. "I don't know, Kim.
It's weird, but it felt kind of good to do a job
well, you know? I was starting to get a kick
out of how clean the pots were getting."

Kim froze. He had to be kidding, but he
sounded serious. "Well, do you want to keep
the job, Jeremy?" she said doubtfully. "I
guess it's good for your moral character or
something."

Jeremy laughed long and hard. Kim was
delighted to see the familiar nasty glint in

his eye. "Are you kidding? My character has had all the uplifting it can take. I'm ready to blow this burger joint for good."

Nikki chatted with Mrs. Burns. She talked to Kevin Hoffman and his sidekick Martin Salko, and she talked to Sasha Lopez. She talked to almost everyone at the party but Tim. He stayed on the other side of the room. If she crossed to get a soda or some pretzels, he immediately moved to the other side.

Then, while Nikki was trying to joke with Kevin, she glanced up and saw Tim dancing with Lara Bennett.

Nikki put her soda down, excused herself, and walked quickly into Mrs. Burns's bathroom. She locked the door, leaned against it, and started to cry. She groped her way to the sink and twisted the taps on to hide the noise of her sobs. How was she ever going to make it through the rest of the evening?

How could she explain everything to Tim? He was so angry with her, but wasn't he wrong, too? He knew she was jealous of Lara, but he didn't discourage the girl. The whole situation was hopeless.

Someone knocked on the bathroom door. "Hey, give someone else a chance!" a voice said.

"Be right out," Nikki called. She filled her hands with cold water and splashed her face.

She looked awful. Quickly she whipped some lipstick out of her purse, but it only made her look paler.

Sighing, she pushed open the door. Whoever had knocked must have gotten tired of waiting. Nikki returned to the living room. There was no sign of Tim or Lara. The music had gotten louder, and the Dead Beats were playing. Mrs. Burns had retreated to the kitchen. Kids were laughing and flirting and eating and dancing. Everyone was in high spirits because the pressure was finally off. Opening night was over, the show had been better the second night, and the matinee on Sunday would be attended mostly by grammar school students and their parents.

Kevin Hoffman walked up behind Nikki. He was still wearing the Stage Manager's hat, and he was grinning. "Dance?" he said loudly over the music.

Nikki shook her head. "No, thanks, Kevin. Maybe later." To her horror, she felt close to bursting into tears again. This was the worst.

Nikki began to push through the crowd, not caring that everyone was staring at her. She ran to the bedroom and rooted through the coats until she found hers. She was terrified someone would see her begin to cry.

Shoving her arms into her coat, Nikki ran for the front door and threw it open. The cool air felt good against her hot cheeks. She started for her car. Luckily it was the last one in the driveway, and no one was blocking her.

She was halfway to the Camaro when she saw them. They were too intent on their conversation to even notice her. Lara was staring up at Tim's face, her skin a blur of white in the darkness. As Nikki watched in horror, Tim slid his arm around Lara's shoulders.

Nikki pressed her knuckles against her mouth to stifle a sob so deep it wrenched her stomach. She started to run, tears streaming down her face, her suede pumps moving soundlessly across the grass.

She threw open the car door and jumped inside, then fumbled with her keys. She had to get out of there!

It must have been the noise of the engine starting that alerted them. As Nikki put the car into reverse and backed out of the driveway, she saw Tim heading across the grass.

He was running toward the car, calling her name. Of course. Tim was an honorable guy. He would want to explain. And the explanation was simple. He'd found the girl who was right for him at last.

Sobbing, Nikki twisted the wheel and put the car into drive. She could hear Tim still calling to her as she stepped on the gas. She wasn't going to listen to his lame explanations! She didn't want to see the pity in his eyes.

She'd have all night to cry, Nikki told herself, as she fiercely wiped her eyes so she could see. But the next day she would have to get up on that stage again. She'd have to show Tim and Lara that she would no longer let her emotions get in the way of her performance. Could she pull it off, though?

As fresh tears ran down her cheeks, Nikki wondered how she could possibly face life without Tim Cooper.

Now that Samantha has met her dream guy, can she get him to help her with more than her French? Karen Jacobs has always been crazy about junior class president Ben Newhouse. Will he ever think of her as more than a friend? Find out in River Heights #6, *Lessons in Love*.

paiving the two of them into slumber…